A Walk Down That Road

A Walk Down That Road

PHILOMENA NGWODO

Copyright © Philomena Ngwodo.

All rights reserved. No part of this book may be reproduced in any form or by any electronic or mechanical means, including information storage and retrieval systems, without permission in writing from the author, except by reviewers, who may quote brief passages in a review.

ISBN: 978-1-64669-664-2   (Paperback Edition)
ISBN: 978-1-64669-665-9   (Hardcover Edition)
ISBN: 978-1-64669-663-5   (E-book Edition)

Some characters and events in this book are fictitious. Any similarity to real persons, living or dead, is coincidental and not intended by the author.

Book Ordering Information

Phone Number: 347-901-4929 or 347-901-4920
Email: info@globalsummithouse.com
Global Summit House
www.globalsummithouse.com

Printed in the United States of America

Chapter 1

It was not yet morning, the event of yester night still left a sharp pain in her broken heart too big to handle. Not knowing where to go or what next to expect, Eliza took a deep breath, shaking with trembling hands and trembling heart. And dark eyes dripping with tears, telling a story, a story of pain, fear and regret which only she could understand perfectly at this moment of her life. She wondered how it all got to this point for her.

Where nothing else seem to matter other than life itself. To the point of no return, notwithstanding the horrible sound coming from the adjacent room from where she was, she tried moving her legs from the dusty floor, but realized she could not. She neither felt life nor pain from trying to move that part of her body. Then she realize she was hurt and dead on that leg! The sharp pain from her back to the leg only made her life worse as that was the beginning of the end for a life full of drama and intrigues. Here she is today, a woman who never considered life to be anything but fun. She would do anything to live forever if that was possible, but today, she has been subjected to the reality of vanity in the face of disaster.

The struggles that have been her life, such stories of a painful troubled life where there was no option or alternative to anything than acceptance of faith to live for the next day, tears, blood and regrets flowed freely from her emotionally wrecked body. Suddenly! She cried out loud," Lord, shine thy face of mercy upon me! Please, don't let this be my last day oh Lord! Help me to be strong, have mercy, OH 'lord! It was like the wakeup call her captors have been waiting for. ''What is wrong with you spoilt brat? I warned you not to make a sound! Do you want me to waste your pretty little body to the vultures in this desert or you want me to kill your baby daughter before your very eye? Chose now! Pointing the gun to her head, ready to kill. Eliza now knew it was not a dream or joking matter anymore. Her captor, devilish looking with large deadly eyes, scuffy looking, smelling bad like a dead rat. He seem not to have a care in the world about anything. Here was a man who probable have seen the worst of life. With no ambition or dreams at all, he looks more ready to die than to live and any attempt to push his button or make him mad, would lead to disaster, not for him, because he has nothing to live for, but for her who love life so much. This gentle brute, Screamed at her saying, 'the choice is yours to stay alive or to die with your daughter! Which do you prefer? This is not the first time she is seeing or hearing this ugly bully who happen to be the same guy whose mood determines what next happens in her shattered life.

Right now, the only thought in her wacked mind is, how to save her 5years old child. She was abducted along with her child when she was just about coming out of her car in front of her friend's house, Rose. Rose is a diplomat and the wife of the city mayor in their little town down the Delta coast of America. She and Eliza's family have been friends for over a decade. Aside from the fact that they are both foreigners and from the same city in America, this friendship extended to the children growing up together and even claiming to be one family. A night before her capture, Rose and Eliza had met in the city mall, just a few kilometers away from the city square, each woman had gone shopping for the usual family monthly food and other house hold supplies.

Rose on her part had a party to organize for the yearly mayor's children end of year show. This is solely her responsibility as the wife of the town mayor, she holds it a duty to host the children of the town every year to lavish party for all. It is an annual tradition which allows her to impact into the lives of all, both rich and poor coming together as one at this time of the year.

While in the shopping mall, Rose was unmindful of the pretty figure standing right behind her, when the cry of a little baby attracted her from the other side of the store. She looked back at the direction of the sound and wondered what type of mother would allow her baby to be crying without attention in such a public mall. At first, she thought to herself, where be the mother of this child, why would she not attend to her baby's needs? She even wondered why any mother can be so uncaring to ignore such high sounding heart wrenching cry of her baby. Why bring her to the mall at this time of the day if she knew the baby would disturb the peace of all in the mall? As far as she is concerned, there are certain things that are better left for nannies or house helps to do. She places every other person below her and likes rating them as second class citizens under her.

Haven come from a very prestigious wealthy family, Rose had never known or seen the other side of midnight or suffering as the case maybe. She have never suffered lack or want, neither has she experience hunger or anything that is unpleasant in her life. Her Irish father and Nigerian mother both met in the United States (US) when both were studying for their doctorate degrees. The mother who worked as a carrier diplomat, ending up in the Nigerian mission House in New York and her father a surgeon who transverse the length and breadth of the world doing what he knows how to do best—(-saving lives)had just three children. Rose was a favorite because she reminded them of their heritage. She has according to her mother, more of her grandmother's fighting spirit and looks physically like her Irish American mother from her father's side. Her Irish grandmother's beauty swept her grandfather off his feet when she was only 17years of age, at that time, she was nick named by her grandfather as one of the Seven Wonders of the World, and her beauty was superb!

Her dad is the product of that love between both, but that was how far their relationship could last. After the birth of her dad, she was told the war broke out in Europe, her grandparents suffered forced separation because her grandfather (God bless his soul) Mr. White man was drafted to the war to fight for his country, he was so proud of his Irish roots that he ended up joining the IRA,(Irish Republican Army).

The IRA fought gallantly against Britain for reasons of war, according to the story, her grandfather won several medals for his country. Her father Richard Whiteman (Jr), was only three (3) years old when his father died fighting for the IRA. They said he flew a jet which was loaded with bombs, fighting through the British no fly zone, his jet was gunned down by the Royal Navy, which ended a very strong love story abruptly with the heart of a young mother forever broken. These memories she kept with her as she struggled alone in her loneliness to raise and save the only fruit of her true love. She left Ireland for America where she successfully raised her only son and child. She was so heart broken and devastated that she refused to be consoled, she never remarried even if she became a forced widow by circumstance at the age of 20years.

The love she had for her late husband, Whiteman (snr), never allowed her to open up her broken heart for another man. She made a promise to Richard (SNR), shortly before he left down the road of no return (War), that she will always and only love him. She promised him also that come rain, come shine, she will die Mrs. Alicia Richard white man senior (srn). Even if she had the premonition of her husband's death, she could not bring herself to the reality when the smartly dressed Army officer pulled up in their little farm house that faithful day, with a crest fallen face and a sober look, holding in his hands the American flag wrapped up nicely and a pair of her husband's cap, he did not finish knocking at the front door when Alicia Richard white man senior and her little son, Richard white man junior, opened and immediately fell down on her kneels sobbing deep from the heart without a sound, but with only hot tears rolling down her pretty innocent face now red from the pain inside. She dreamt about his crash in the jet the previous night in her sleep.

Henry willow did not think this was going to be easy for him, in fact, he regretted this part of his military life to the end. The thought of you been a messenger of doom or disseminator of bad news to close friend's wife or family is worse than you bombing a million enemy camps for him. But this was a task that must be accomplished for two reasons- to be closer in time of needs and to discharge your duties to father land, whether good or bad, you are to obey before complain, orders must be obeyed. That day was one very bad day for this young officer who has just lost his partner who was more of a family to him.

Sometimes in our lives, we are our own worst enemies, the fear of our own self is worse than that of an enemy in certain circumstances of our lives. This heaviness he carried as he drove down the road to the home of a young widow and her little son who knows not what tomorrow holds for them.

Henry willow hart had been a very close friend of the white man's, he has been a good friend of Alicia parker even before she became Mrs. Alicia Richard white man senior after her marriage to Richard, in fact, Richard met his wife through henry's sister who was a friend. Henry knew what the sad news would do to Alicia whose dodged spirit and desire to live and die, if possible in Richard senior's arms would have made her go back to her creator in peace, but fate dealt a big blow to that wish.

Henry could not bring himself to easily break this sad news to her and her three years old boy who was obviously looking helplessly at his mother's sobbing red face. Alicia's thought quickly switched over to her little son who looked up growing under the tutelage of a responsible, disciplined life with his loving father whose patriotism and love for his country, supersedes any other. '' I am so, so sorry Alicia, I wish I can make this moment easy for you, but I can only imagine life for you and little Richard without his father. I do wish to stand by you whenever you need me. He did love you so much. I will always be here if you need a shoulder to cry on, trust me Alicia, I will never abandon you and his son. That is a promise' 'Alicia could not utter a word, all she could do was to fizzle out into the emptiness of her future without the one true love of her life. She wondered if a man can just be taken away just like that under the twinkle of an eye without notice, then she thought death has dealt her a terrible blow, too strong to overcome. Her thought went to her little innocent son who will never know the love and care of a father like she did enjoy as a child or even know the scent or smell of his father as he trod through the different stages of his life.

The greatest of all her worries is haven to raise him all alone, this was the most painful aspect of it all. Unfortunately, Alicia was alone, fully and truly unprepared for what destiny entrusted on her tender little lap. But the thought of raising a son whose image of his father is the tonic she desires to face whatever vicissitudes of life challenges made her develop into a very strong woman over night for a new life without, love, comfort, full of uncertainties and more of worries, but that must be successful for her and her son. She then vowed to raise her son with so much love, value and sense of responsibility. With fairness to all in his life, and justice for all, but above all, with love and respect for women, no matter what. Hard as it seems, it is to her a task that must be accomplished in honor of the man she truly loved.

Alicia started out as a baker, her baking business started out of the little money she had saved before the death of her husband. It grew so successful, making her so popular in her community that many wondered if she was born a baker, this is a talent she hid when her husband was alive. Her confectionary business was always a first choice both for the high and low in the society. She succeeded so well that giving her son, Richard junior a sound education wasn't so difficult.

She sent him to schools in the very best of the best in the world and she was very proud of his many successes in his chosen carrier before her death at the age of 55years of ovarian cancer. One thing that Richard keep wondering about his mum until her death was the kind of love she expressed and carried in her heart for his late father. A man he never knew in person, but felt very close to from the stories his mother told him. He wondered if such love could still be found in this modern day women and prayed God to give him as a wife, a woman as loving, honest and hardworking as his mother when it was time to walk down that road of his life. Unfortunately, he grew up to marry an opposite. Carol, his diplomat lawyer wife is the direct opposite of his mother or anything good in a woman in most ways. The only similarity between his wife and his late mother, is the doggedness and strong fighting spirit for excellence and success in whatever they do. And this was the quality he saw in her 20years ago, when they met in Harvard University in the United States of America.

Although, he did not take time to study or look beyond the beauty of the tiny pretty girl who was always tops in her class without regard for any of her male colleagues. He was beclouded with her beauty and intelligence so much so that he forgot to look out for the telltale signs of the disaster of his marriage. He did not look out for the right signs for a successful marriage. She is so pompous of her aristocratic background and allowed it to get into her head so much that she neglected the basic things in her marriage to Richard Whiteman junior. Carol became unbearable as a wife to him, so bad and a pain in the ass to her husband and children to the extent they were just living or co-habiting for the sake of the children. She lives on the fast lane of life while Richard still remembers the son of whom he is and where he is coming from before getting to an unknown destination in life. Richard knew so well what he had gotten into after the birth of their first child Sam. Before Sam's birth, carol pretended to be the humble perfect wife, selfless, caring and very romantic.

A woman who loves her family dearly, mostly her husband. But all this changed for her when she highly connected political father, secured a high paying job for her in the mission house also in New York as the Diplomatic legal officer for the mission. Soon, she started her globetrotting all over the world in the name of working hard at the detriment of her marriage and home.this is truly the mistake most successful working class carrier women make. She would sometimes go away to work in the morning and never return home until after two weeks or sometimes two months on the roll!

All she does when she leaves is drop her family a note, as for her, calling her husband or children on the phone is too time wasting for her. whenever she comes back, after the family and marital abandonment, "SORRY" is just too expensive for her to offer anyone. This is because she believes that with her father's wealth and connections, everyman will be too happy to have her as a friend or wife. The world to her, is at her feet! Even if she trample on any man, she believes he should be happy to take her insults, her spoilt upbringing contributed to her wrong perceptions of life as well as her bad judgments of others. She can't help who she is at all. This fact she is unaware of, carol sees herself as the only perfect person in this world who is not to be challenged or ignored. She is the one who must be obeyed!

She cannot stand anyone challenge her actions or person, even when she is mostly wrong, carol claims to be right, she is identified with anything argue mental. Both her husband and children see this trait as a big embarrassment to the family reputation. Nobody, but herself see how perfect and unique she is, people often wondered how Richard Whiteman junior copes with such a rude silly, spoilt brat! They see him as a man enslaved and blinded by his genuine love for his wife! His mother brought him up to always love and respect women, no matter what, Richard white man junior will never say anything negative about his wife to anyone. He will always defend her before the world but how far have this attitude helped the marriage is yet to be determined, as for carol her public image can never be compromised for anything else. She would prefer to sacrifice her family for her carrier and public image can never be compromised for anyone.

Richard Whiteman (JR) always wondered in his heart if his dear mother whom he so much loved and worshiped, if she would have been able to withstand the type of wife her dear son ended up with, he wondered what life would have been for him and how unhappy and terribly heart broken his late mum would have been to see her only child and dear son, whom she raised with so much love suffer this terrible pain silently and lonely in his adult life from the hand of a woman! What would she have done, what would she have advised me to do? He wondered silently as he looked helplessly trapped! Despite all his prayers and efforts, Richard is now fully convinced more than ever before, that God is not kind to him in the choice of wife he gave him!

He say to her severally, that she is the only failure and biggest regret of his life! The greatest mistake of his life! The only thing he did wrong in his life and the only thing bad about his life that he cannot change or do nothing about for certain reasons! Regretfully for many, having a wife who falls short of giving love and attention to the family, is worse than living with someone you hardly ever know! For Richard Whiteman junior, carol falls short of his expectation of a decent wife, the type he saw in his mother who built in him the desire to respect any woman, no matter how horrible she turns out to be in character or looks. For Richard, obviously, his late mother will be turning in her grave from the anger of seeing her dear son suffer so much pain. Could this woman, and his choice of a wife be his greatest undoing that could destroy everything he believes in and everything his mother taught him to respect and hold on to? Time will surely tell!

Chapter 2

For Richard, life without carol is like living a life of emptiness, he has to make up his mind whether to continue in this bondage called marriage or free himself from the brink of death in this marriage with carol, the biggest problem is disappointing his late mother whom he cherish so much in life and death even if it means doing what he should not, to keep this promise is a big burden, to break this promise is certainly inevitable, but to take a step towards fulfilling a shattered life in the hands of a woman, so loved, so cherished packed with so many countless heartaches and traumas of a sinking life. And dying away with the setting sun is another matter for a tomorrow that is so uncertain for him!

Stepping out of her hotel into the early morning sun, with the dimly light sky and the warm air from the sky in Kenya, carol did not bother to put up her hand to cover the opening in between the lap of the flower gown she was wearing that day. With the weather warm and windy, haven spend close to a week outside her home without a single call to Richard or the children. What was uppermost in her mind was the 2pm appointment between her and the president of the Kenya business community, suddenly, a tall handsome dark haired guy, approached from behind," may I help with your papers and any other thing you want me to"? She turned back to see who it was not knowing why she did that, but she turned anyway to see. The handsomeness of what stood before her, made her lose her composure for once in her life.

This is such a handsome man she thought to herself. How I wish he would bow to my dirty command as others before him in my life, she smiled priggishly without care to what it means, this gentle man mistook this as an open invitation for him to conquer another of his women, and he miss took her smiles as the tonic for his new adventure in Kenya. To him, carol is too sexy to let go, maybe his charisma would do the magic for him. Looking lost in their dirty thought towards each other, carol stood still, it's like her world came to a stop momentarily because of the raw handsome gentleman standing so close to her now.

Gentleman, so handsome and so sweet to resist even for a woman like her who never sees anything good in anyone, but this one is different. She never expected any man to have such effect or boldness to approach her, talk less of a guy who is barely able to give her the world and its good things which of course from her assessment from his simple looks, he could have been another of the hotels staff. Worst still, the dark haired guy repeated his request with a disarming charm and sexy bedroom baritone voice.

His eyes raving through her body as someone staved of sex for a period of time, he said' 'what a cute lady you are! I guess you could do with a little help with those files of yours before the wind blows them all off. Am Dean, stretching out his hairy long arms to shake hers, what is your name? She did not know what compelled her to shake his hands or even give him her name but she, unlike her, responded by taking his hand, saying" I'm carol Richards Whiteman, please to meet you. Dean have penchant for dating highly sophisticated society women. He finds it challenging and the more challenging it is to him, the more fun he gets. It is fun for him to get in between the sexy laps of these women, either married or single, he really does not care provided you appeal to his taste and desire. This to him is a way of looking down on them and demystifying their ego. He believes these set of women, to a large extent, look down on their husbands or men in their lives because of the power they have.

They see themselves as the beginning and the end of the world. Though he is charming and wealthy, but never married or loved any woman truly before in his life, with all his wealth and connections. He believes that a man needs to exhaust, extend and express his manhood properly as much as he can before settling down to a perpetual life of faithfulness with a woman of his own. Can we walk down this road together? He asked carol who by now is still trying to make sense out of this situation. 'Oh, sure but I am just on my way to the hotel mall to pick up a few items for my 2pm appointment later in the day with a business partner. Are you a business woman or what? I'm a diplomat lawyer, but why all this question from a stranger like you? He winked at her with a grimy smile on his face, sorry to ask but I am not a stranger to you carol. Do you mind if I call you by your first name? Sure, I do. I am married, in case you refuse to notice the ring on my finger and I am equally late for my meeting. He smiled and said" the ring does not make the home or marriage, but the individual and their actions or in actions do my dear angel" at this time, they were both close to the entrance door of the hotel mall when she stretch out her hand and collected her files he was carrying from him and briskly walk away into the back dusty alleys of the Kenya stores all lined up on the streets. Surely, this guy has an effect on her she wondered inside why so.

Hi, I don't bite! Can I see you again? She did not even bother to look back at him but she only waved him off with the back of her hand as usual of her. She would rather concentrate on what she was going to tell Mr. Kanga, chairman of Kenya chamber of business community. Mr. Kanga has been on carols target list for a long time business wise. He is the very traditional African man who finds it sometimes very repulsive and rebellious for a woman to be in a man's position. He particularly detest carols guts because he sees her as a snobbish spoilt brat who have no regard for anybody, mostly the specie call men.

As far as Mr. Kanga is concerned, a woman like carol in Africa should not see the light of day in the busy world of politics or diplomacy. She should be relegated to the kitchen background preparing delicious meals and delicacies for the family, the best is for her to be seen only when she comes out to entertain her husband's friends when necessary. She should be tending to the children's needs and at night, dutifully warm her husband's bed anytime he wants. On the contrary, carol's hatred for Mr. Kanga in particular started a long time ago when the Kenya Ambassador visited New York where carol is the mission diplomat lawyer for her country, kanga was among the Ambassador's delegate when they organized a dinner party, after the business meeting between both countries in honor of the Ambassador and his entourage.

On that faithful day, carol was her best in hurting people. She was the chief organizer of the event, equally out to show off as usual, but unfortunately for her, the likes of kanga cannot stand a bitchy' lady like her. He is one of the few African men who still dwell in the past, that the kitchen is the rightful place for a women. He believes that a woman is to be seen but not to be heard! Well, he was not prepared for the likes of carol in his life, she stepped on his toes towards the end of the event, and it was time for the final toast and the presentation of gifts to the Ambassador and his entourage. It was carol who stepped forward to touch the gift recklessly, earlier, kanga noticed she was the first to go to the table to serve herself food even before it was time for it. She it was at the wine table that drank from a bottle of wine before the very eye of all. The Ambassador and his guest were still exchanging pleasantries, when kanga noticed the lady breaking all decent rules. And now again, the same lady is committing another crime as far as he is concerned. He felt it was time to put her in her place. Although, other guest noticed the lady's uncultured attitude, but turned a blind eye to it because of who she is.

Those who know her were not surprised, but her visitors, among whom is kanga were not at all happy. 'How dare you woman, how can you be so uncultured to touch anything on that table before the men here? I don't care who or what you are, but this is totally unacceptable where I come from!

In Africa, women are not allowed that, they are only meant to be seen serving guest at this kind of occasion and not to be heard or be in control, this to me is an abomination in my culture. But to his and other people's greatest shock, carol stood her ground, she quietly replied kanga thus" Mr. Kanga, I am truly sorry to know that your ancient type of men still exist. I am also sorry for your women back in your country who still put up with ancestors like you, but I am not too sorry to disappoint you because this is America, a land of freedom and opportunities where women are not only seen, heard, respected and valued! Here, women rule and rock! When you get back to Africa, please do me a favor, free your women from slavery or bondage, love and respect them for whom God has made them to be. Not the weaker sex as you think, but the power behind the force of you and every man!" It is a free world sir! Still holding on to her glass of red wine, she turned back and continued feeding herself to the delicacies on the table.

Both kanga, the visiting Ambassador and all others left in bewilderment! They all could not believe the drama unfolding before their very eyes, it was like putting iron into hot fire to roast the ass of an enemy for kanga. The incident still lingers in his memory, it triggers something in him, sometimes he feels African women truly deserves better from their men. He remembers his early life as a young teacher in a village school where he fell in love for the first time with a 16years old student in his class. Ada, was a shy girl from a village adjacent to kanga's, she had gotten pregnant by him and he bluntly refused to acknowledge or accept responsibility.

Even when he knew he was responsible, he denied Ada and the pregnancy, she was eventually sent out of school expelled and banished from her home to suffer alone. Kanga never bothered to find out what happened to her or the pregnancy after then. But the events of those early reckless wickedness of his, keep hunting his life. If ever Ada gave birth to the child, whether the child is a male or female alive or dead, he does not know or seem to care. This is because the men of Africa get away easily with such abuse to the women. They are never seen to be at fault in such circumstance, but always the careless ones who crave for sex when they shouldn't is the women considered to be.

Mr. Kanga never came out of that regret, most times in his sleep, he sees images of what the child looked like, and he imagines it in the image of his other children now. That is a secret of his past he does not want awakened or exposed, but he craves for answers as he also begs God for forgiveness. Carols words brought back that same guilt for him in a stronger way, he knows that African women are truly in need of freedom from some harsh cultural believes which holds them bondage from true realities of the modern times. Carol has succeeded in waking up the ghost of his past. What can he do now? " maybe one day I will see Ada to apologize, maybe I will see my child too and reconcile before God calls me home in death. I have to make amends. She has a point, I must admit that much to myself, but I am still an African man with great pride". As kanga sat down in deep thoughts, pensive and alone, this incident still lingering in his memory until his second meeting again with carol, but this time around, carol would do anything possible to win his (kanga) country trade support which would give her a major boost at work.

It is a very challenging and ironic situation that could leave her ego bruised and deflated, depending on the outcome of this meeting with the man she had earlier humiliated back in New York. Mr. Kanga have great influence and high respect of his people. As a leader, he is one of the few men who dwell in a dual capacity of holding on to the ancient cultural believes as well as the modern times when dealing with situations.

He has the ears of the president and top politicians of his country with the love and respect of his people. But the greatest challenge for carol in this mission is how to approach and convince this man to see her as a changed person and give her what she wants. Now in kanga territorial net, needing help from him for her country to gain all the international trade in that zone. She knew it is not in her character to bow down to anybody or beg, talk less a man like kanga!

Where or how will she start this story? Is it by apologizing sincerely for her supposed stupidity or for telling him she is in-charge of affairs where she rules her world? Is it the fact that she has never accepted to be wrong in whatever she does right from her pampered childhood days which still lingers in her clumsy mind?? Well! A task that must be accomplished, must be accomplished! She said to herself, voicing out aloud "lord, let this cup pass me by" she prayed.

For the first time in a long time, carol found herself praying to god! She never prays over anything before because she had it all, or so she thought. Until now, everything was going as planned, why do I have to face this man of all people at this time? I should have known better, this African man, most of them know nothing but bullying and insulting their poor women. But is it a must at all for me to go to this meeting today? What can I do not to lose my pride before this man? I should seek immediate help, if he is to humiliate anybody, definitely not me, she concluded with those words.

She got into the shower, took her bath hurriedly and jumped back into her room to dress up. After about a few minutes inside the room, a thought flashed through her mind. Yes', I must not fall down completely before this African man, I can still pull this, I got to go look for somebody I will use as a bait to do this dirty job with kanga before I face him, but first, I must postpone this 2pm meeting until I get my perfect guy. She called kanga office he was not there but she left a message with the secretary asking her to please inform her boss she would not be able to keep up with the appointment for that day and to ask for another appointment date for next week.

Grace have been working for kanga for almost a decade. She could read him like the back of a book but in matters like this, she knew her boss's hatred for eccentric American woman called carol or 'Madam America' by her boss. She was instrumental to this first appointment in the first place because carol was able to relate better with Grace who likes the good things of life like carol. Whenever she can, carol buys gifts for most secretaries of different countries she visits thereby building a relationship bond she could use anytime necessary to her advantage. In this particular case, Grace knew that it would be an uphill task to convince her boss kanga to give carol another appointment easily. In her mind, she knew that kanga's conclusion on this cancellation would be seen as another of (madam Americas') carol's dirty pride again. As it is, she ensured that she chose the perfect time to tell Mr. Kanga of the cancellation and a rescheduled date she secured for carol as she looks forward to another gold wrist watch from the American woman whenever possible.

A date was fixed for a week from now. Back in the hotel, carol stepped out into the lobby seeking and hoping desperately to find Dean. Of all her thought, the tall dark haired guy took the better part of her. What she cannot understand is the way her body responds to this selfish thought for a stranger she hardly knew, a stranger that would later play an important role in her life. Luckily for her, as she sat down in the bar to sip from her glass of red wine, a tall shadow walked by, to her surprise, she looked up, and it was dean sitting opposite her table.

'Hi there, he walked up to her table, do you mind if I join you for a drink? Oh, oh' not at all, please do sit down. So, we meet again my cute angel. Yes sure today is your lucky day Dean. Carol was not too comfortable sitting with Dean so close. She was sweating, losing her composure once again before this total stranger. She felt something she had never felt before for any man in her life, it was like butterflies moving in her stomach all before a total stranger who only concentrated in her sexy blue eyes a heritage of her Irish background. Can we talk as friends? She was hesitant, but had no choice because, this could be the only perfect guy to accomplishing her mission with kanga." Sure, you can call me by my first name carol, may I call you by yours too? 'Yes, sure call me Dean.

Nice to meet you once more Dean, same here carol. They both shook hands while smiling at each other as they speak looking straight into each others eyes. Shall I order for you, what is your preference please? I like scotch on the rock please. Ok, we are in the same club, just a minute then. He dashed to the other corner of the dimly lit bar to fetch them drinks, at the back of his mind, Dean wondered what a great fortune he had today. He could not get the thought of haven met carol earlier in the day outside the hotel. The evasive and sexy nature left a deep feeling to conquer this lady in Dean's mind, it was to him, a mission that must be accomplished.

He followed his instinct to come down stairs that afternoon hoping to find her, if only to catch a glimpse of this rude sexy American lady he likes. Now the chicken has come home to roost and the goat has entered into the lion's den so to speak! As he settles the two glass of drink on the table, Dean knew how not to let a life time opportunity as this slip away. He promised himself that he would get deeply into the head, heart and bury himself in the life of this rude sexy one without looking back on the possible consequences if and when it eventually back fires! Are you here for business? Yes, I came for a business meeting and I am not too sure how to go about it. What do you mean by that? Well, I 'm not too sure, but I am having problem meeting with the person I am to see. She said, looking worried and confused. And why is that? Well, Mr. Kanga is a very difficult old man, I think he has particular penchant for hating educated women. I'm sorry, but that is just my own opinion of him, he seems too African and too traditional for my liking. I wonder how he manages to be the head of such an international body all these years.

'Wow, wow, are you talking about Mr. Kanga, the same kanga that we all know here in Kenya? Aye, do you know him? Sure, he is one of the best friends I have here in Kenya and I respect him so much, I quiet agree with you on that. He is truly African, one of the few African men who still dwell in the past, certainly, Mr. Kanga will not like a very sexy, educated and free spirited woman like you, but that aside, I can help you, that is- if you want me to, but...........he stopped short of saying the words when carol quickly jumped at his offer of assistance with kanga. Oh, that would be very great for me.

It's like you read my mind Dean, I could not make my appointment with him by 2pm today because I don't know how to face a man like that without flaring up again. By this time, Dean was mindful of her use of language, how do you mean? Do you have any problem with him? He asked because of the way she was talking, looking straight into her eyes again, she tried not to look back at his intent sexy gaze. Ok, if you don't want to talk about it, I understand, please take your drink. She fumbled with the glass in her hand, not knowing how to respond to telling Dean the truth about her previous encounter with kanga or to still at this point remain silent.

She only want to use Dean Break kanga's pride in getting what she wants. The greatest challenge to her is still how to use this guy for her dirty job. Dean is an important man to carol at this point in time, he is not to be offended or disposed of just like that by her because she needs him. While the spirit is willing not to fall for him, the flesh is certainly weak, so it seems! She yielded to the demands of the sinful flesh, her sudden lust and this craving of the flesh for a total stranger whom she cannot do away with for now, is a taste in her life! Oh' no! Please, do spend some time with me, do you mind if we go up to my room now? She invited him to her room without knowing why she did that, even if she knew it was dangerous for her to do so. It's like inviting a sex starved man into the same bedroom with a drunken sleeping naked lady whose triangle section between her two legs is spread wide open facing the sex starved man at night! But that is just what he was looking or praying for right from the first time he set his eyes on her. To him, having carol in-between his sheets is another feather to his cap, he will certainly conquer this woman, no matter what! Ok, I don't mind at all joining you upstairs, he said with a glow in his eyes as they both walked side by side to the 5th floor of the prestigious Royal chart hotel, owned by the famous chart family whose large investment concerns spread all through Asia, America, Europe and Africa.

Inside the elevator, carol could see through her inner self, that part of her which crave for a faithful marriage vow to Richard white man (JR), but the other part of her was secretly dying for an unholy adventure with this stranger! Ever since her child hood days back at New York, she has always gotten what she wanted by any means possible, a character trait that is today her greatest undoing. She is willing to extend her nuisance complex to this new world of infatuation, believing what her body tells her instead of holding on to what her heart says.

Dean stretch out his right arm, gently placing it across her tiny shoulder, hoping she would initially resist this subtle love advance from him. But the confusion and spur of the moment did not give her the power to resist him or realize that for the first time, a stranger as it were, have deflated her sexual mechanism, so easily without her resisting. Even Richard her husband did not get her so easily on a platter of gold like this, she lean backwards to his right shoulder, resting her small frame on his masculine body, wow! This is the right moment! Dean have been waiting for this, he thought to himself that, to let this woman go is a mistake, rather, he will let her know how passionate he can be with matters of the heart.

At the initial stage of most of his crazy relationships, Dean is always every woman's dream of the perfect man. He gives the maximum attention to any woman that is his targeted prey until he finally gets between her two legs in bed! The triangle section in between the woman's legs is his ultimate target, it is the only thing he craves desperately from the previous women, even for carol too. It is after tasting the forbidden apple of the triangle zone, then he shows the women the dark side of his life, if and only when he is truly satisfied with the prey. Sometimes, he wonders if he will ever find a place in his heart to truly love a woman and settle down with one woman, make babies with her and remain faithful to her for the rest of his life!

He smiled gently at carol, he supported and settled her shaking body on his, now she is sweating from the heat of passion and desires of the flesh. He could feel her heart beat, racing fast in between her succulent breast which nipples are pointing out hard like a pointed love arrow fired by cupid straight to a lover's heart!

The elevator came to a halt on the 5th floor, the door opened in the lobby, Dean's name was called by someone from the other end from a sweet female voice. As he turned around to see who it was, he saw Phil. Phil is one of the numerous unfortunate conquered targets of Dean's past. She fell for him 4years ago, he slept with her, left her high and dry in the cold hotel room one winter night. Ever since, Phil have not set eyes on this handsome Casanova only for her to see him today in the hands of another prey. They both exchange quick glances, she looking at him with so much hate and him trying to cover up his act with a big smile and good words for Phil, hello Dean, 'oh, hi Phil, what brings you here? He ask as if he does not know already. 'I came for business and pleasure as usual you know. Are you staying or you are visiting a friend like me? I can see your hands are full again, you never miss a target! She grin at him with carol wondering what was going on between them. Meet carol my good friend. Carol, meet Phil my old friend. Please to meet you Phil, same here carol. Well, we should be going, see you around.

Dean quickly walked by her towards the direction of carols room. He had earlier in the day made enquires to find out details about carols lodgment in the hotel from the room boy. He knew that if he stays a moment longer, Phil could expose him and spoil his chance. His sexual weapon has already risen to the occasion after all those sexual touching between him and carol inside the elevator. Who is that lady? Carol ask him. She is just an old friend of mine back in the days, nothing to worry about, he replied. I see. I hope I'm not stepping on anybody's toes? Not at all my angel, for you I will climb the highest mountains without ropes or shoes! Smiling, holding closer to her as they walk.

You only is very free to possess this body, opening the door to her room for carol to enter as he speaks. After you my angel, smiling, back inside the room carol quickly walked to her mini bar wondering if it was the right thing to do. Haven seen the weakness and helplessness of her body, the coldness in Phil's eyes when she spoke to Dean outside the lobby, she suspected that Dean is been economical with the whole truth as far as all the information regarding the pretty lady is concerned. What can I offer? She ask him. He was busy cursing the strange encounter with Phil.

He resolved to deny any further question concerning that issue, should carol make any further attempt to ask him. There is every possibility for him to have his way again with this bigger fish if and only when he plays his cards right. He thought to himself, unknown to him, carol have her own plans to use him serve her selfish purpose with Mr. Kanga, the greatest obstacle in her carrier right now. I would have a tout of vodka on ice please, but if you don't mind, you can give without ice. 'Oh, I do have what you want right here, I was just about serving that, carol retorted. It has always been a choice for me aside red wine. I take it whenever I'm tensed up like this. You, tensed up? Dean asked surprisingly, even when he knew in his heart of heart that this strong woman seems depressed and troubled!

As a matter of fact, Dean knew that he could not have the opportunity of coming this close to her room, let alone sharing such intimate time together if all had been normal with her. He stood behind her tiny frame, the heat from her warm body heating up the sexual demon more and more in him. Don't stop me please, don't allow this moment die, carol, I have great respect for you. I am not taking advantage of you or this moment in history, but I'm sorry, I can't help myself, I can't help this feelings I have inside for you. Since the first time we saw, I have not been myself, I have dreamt of moments like this all night as I sleep. He pressed his body harder and closer to hers, holding her trembling hands and shaking body, but she gathered whatever is remaining of her pride or dignity to push Dean away from her weak body, still pretending not to want him! 'Oh, sorry Dean, I don't understand anymore.

After remembering what she wanted him for with kanga, she forced those words out of her mouth moving slowly away. You don't understand what carol? Are you feeling something for me or you love me already? She laughed at this questions from Dean hysterically, ha, ha! Ha!! I'm sorry to laugh like that, please do not take it otherwise, I just cannot believe what is happening right now. Can I say that I do find you very, very attractive but I am truly sorry this is not the right thing to do right now? Let us face the business at hand, I am troubled with how to get kanga approval for my country more than anything else right now, do excuse me please. She dropped her sexy bracelet Dean had earlier taken off her neck and made her way straight to the balcony of her beautiful hotel room. Leaving the gentleman hanging with hungry sexual desires desperately.

Chapter 3

Back at home, Richard white man (JR) sat down alone in the spacious beautifully decorated apartment with nothing but the thought of his family. He wondered how his wife carol degenerated to this point in the marriage, the idea of an ideal home which he grew in as a child did not turn out to be his in this twist of fate with his marriage to carol. Could it be my fault, is it a mistake in my life to have married this woman, the one true love of my life? Did I overlook something's I should have considered in the choice of wife I married? All this thoughts racing in his head, suddenly, he realized a shadow was right in front of him standing hands akimbo looking straight at him. He never realized the presence standing before him until he felt the cool breeze blowing across his face from the shadow standing in his presence. Daddy, what is going on with you? April is the first daughter and the second child of the Whiteman's. She have always been the vocal one in the family, an extrovert who never misses an opportunity to talk on any issue she wants.

She knew her father was not happy the way her mother is behaving, she knew the game her mother is playing with her father and character wise, she knew her mother is zero! She keep hoping that all will be well someday between her parents even when things seem to truly fall apart with the center not holding waters, she is still hoping that the strong love her father have for her mother(which to her is a family tradition), should be able to make things better for them. Unknown to her, in her father's mind, this family tradition is under threat, it is no longer at ease with a man who have suffered untold hardship emotionally and otherwise, total neglect and abuse for the better part of this relationship from his wife, carol. Can this family tradition as it were truly save this non-existent or living dead marital union? God almighty is the only one that can save carols marriage to Richard at this point in time.

" Daddy, what is going on, why are you sitting here all alone? You are not smiling daddy, what is the matter? She sat down on her father's laps on the sofa in their living room apartment as usual, holding out a bouquet of flower with the right hand towards her father. This came for you this morning. I wonder who is sending my father flowers, daddy, are you seeing someone else behind mothers back? Are you unfaithful to mum? Hell no, why on earth do you think I can ever cheat on your mother! I can never cheat on her, even if she hasn't been there for me in this marriage all these years, she has not really been much of a wife or mother to any of us in this house, anyway.

I know all is not perfect between us now, but I am very optimistic she will soon come to her senses, that is not an excuse for any of us to be unfaithful or stupid. I'm raised to love and respect women, even when they are the worst of all creatures sometimes. Sorry, I said that I'm just too tired my child, I need to go to bed now if you will excuse me. He got up and walked helplessly with tears rolling down his eyes into the dark of the night shutting the massive door to their bedroom, he emptied himself into his lonely bed, sobbing uncontrollably like a little baby who just lost his precious mother! He disappeared into the enclave of the comfort of his loneliness, wallowing in pain and regrets.

This loneliness that have become thick darkness, engulfing his entire existence so to speak. To say April is shocked to see and hear all those hurting words from a father she so love and who loves her mother carol to death, is an amazing understatement of facts. April could not move herself away from the sofa, so far, she have just come face to face with the reality of accepting the axiom that 'love alone is not enough to hold a marriage together in the face of trails and temptations that is life threatening. Us humans, have a lot to contribute towards the success or failures of our marriages. No matter the level we may have attained in life and society, be it academically, socially, financially, educationally and otherwise. Our character, actions and inactions makes a whole lot of difference in the success or failures of our homes and lives'. She did not know whether to go console her father, call mother to come quickly back home because there seem to be a very big crack already in this illusively solid perfect home!

'God, where is mum? Her home is falling apart! I hope she comes back to meet the remnant or the fragment of a once perfect home?" So my poor daddy have been carrying all this mountain of problems on his shoulders alone? Yet, he still pretends all is well and gives us the best to make us happy? I respect this father of mine! She knew her daddy would not want to discuss anything with either her or anyone else except the woman he married. And this woman is not the type that cares if one dies or lives as long as she is comfortable and getting what she wants as and whenever necessary.

In his mind, the urge to do away with carol is stronger than staying to salvage a dead marriage, again the training he got from his late mother, Alicia, and the promise made to himself and his dear mother, cannot be easily broken! What about his children, what would they say of him as a father? How would they live their lives knowing mummy and daddy have gone their separate ways? Richard Whiteman (JR), what is the way out for you?

Early the next morning, April went to knock on her father's bedroom door, all through the night, the thought of a broken family and a father with a wounded heart kept her from having a good night sleep. Good morning daddy, can I come in to see you please? She did not hear any response from the inside of her father's room. Hi, Mr. Richard Whiteman (JR), can your little angel daughter come kiss her father good morning please? Anything to make him happy at this moment is what she will do. After seeing what she saw last night, not knowing how else to make her father know she understand more than he could ever imagine what he was going through, April felt responsible towards helping her father find joy like he once knew. Not now, he finally answered. Daddy, please let me come in. if you don't open this door, I will just sit down here and I will not eat, drink or go to school, until I see my daddy. 'Ok, ok! I will open for you little devil. He open the door with the heaviness of his heart from the previous night still in his eyes, Richard pretended to hide that pain and agony he is suffering from before his daughter.

But it is not working, 'I know daddy this is none of my business, I know I am just a little sweet devil, but I am sure I love both my parents. The pain of anyone of you is also my pain as is the joy of both of you, my joy also, why are you so sad? His head bent downwards, tears rolling down his check again, Richard did not know how to explain to his daughter what it was that he is truly going through. He does not want to hurt or poison her innocent mind about anything. But he also knew that she is too intelligent to be lied to and be ignored with a wave of the hand. At that tender age of 15years, April can be described as a re-incarnated ancestor who have come to cement the broken walls and holes in the lives of these two strange bed fellows.

Where and how can he start his story without touching the sensitivity of this sentimental saint whose mind should not at this time be polluted with the many troubles of his adult life? Well, my angel, your father is passing through difficult times, I would need you to try and understand daddy, give daddy a little privacy to suffer this nightmare of his life alone. And now, who made you a psychologist? When did you become a mind reader, how come you think you know all that goes on in dad's adult life? I would advise you to leave adults to solve their problems themselves.

He kissed her little cheeks and got up from the bed to take a shower. No daddy, you are looking for an escape route, it is not going to be easy for me to tell my dear daughter the pain I am passing through. Richard cannot understand himself in this marriage. He knows if he opens up to his daughter, he will certainly betray the promise and trust he made to his late mother. Must he die in silence for the love he has for his wife? Deep down, the answer to this nightmare rest with him alone, only he can save himself from this dark life where he now finds himself. He stood under the shower tap in his bathroom, turned on the water and sobbed once more like the lost soul he is. If only he had taken time to study the disaster his marriage turned out to be, his wife, carol did all she could to put everyone in the family under her authority without Richard stopping her, he was too blinded by his love for her to see her faults. Stepping out from the bath room, he did not bother to open the bedroom door for the day, he only reclined on his bed and slept off deeply in his anguish since it was a weekend. As for his daughter April, noticing this danger in her parents' marriage is not enough, she will have to do something if the marriage will ever survive to help.

But as it is, her mother is neither bothered, she is not the type that would even listen to her if she decides to confide in her the pain her father is going through in their marriage. All she knows and cares for, is making more successes out of her diplomatic carrier, this is more important to her than family life. Sometimes in our lives, fate takes us round several roads in life, some good, others bad. It gives to those who don't deserve, more than those who desires, but what can one do, who can question the wisdom in God's sharing formulas? Such is the case with this eccentric woman who only craves for her own satisfaction even when God in his infinite kindness gave her a good home to love and manage to his glory. Where on earth is my mother? April, ask.

Things cannot continue like this in this house, I have to reach my mum one way or the other. She quickly dressed up for school that morning, rushed out to catch the first school bus to school. In the high school where she is, April is known as the extroverted daughter of a rich family whose mother is very nasty. She has more of her father's humility and humble spirit, more than the indifference of her nasty mother.

Until now, nothing ever bothered this tom-boy' daughter of the Richards. As the events of last night between her and her dad flash through her mind, she thought it wise to seek the advice of her close friend in school that day. Hello Joseph. Hi April, you look great! Oh, thanks anyway. Are you heading for class or you are free to talk? I have class by 1pm, for now, I'm all yours, April. Smiling childishly as he held her arms in his and they walked to a corner to sit down talking. Ok, can we sit and talk for a while please? Sure girl, anything for a sweet devil like you. They both sat down under the sycamore tree behind the class block in the school. She was silent for a few seconds before speaking, I'm having this feeling all is not well with my parent's relationship. I know my mum is the problem, but I'm worried my dad could be suffering in silence for the love he has for my mum.

Sometimes, I think my dad is foolishly in love with a woman who does not deserve that kind of love. I think his love is completely senseless and unimaginative as I would want to describe it. I have never in my little life seen a man so dedicated to his believes in love and family to the extent of suffering so much shame in neglect, even in the face of many. I only hope and pray for my father to be able to differentiate stupidity from values of true love if truly there is anything close to that between him and mom. All I know is that someday, dad will set himself free from this torture he calls true love. I 'm deeply affected by this all my friend." Hi, what is going on in your ancient mind again? You talk as if the world between your parents' have fallen apart more than imagined. April, I do hope you are not getting too involved with adult troubles? Your dad is old enough and wise enough to know when to take off the pinching shoes. If really he feels he is wearing one, I sincerely hope you are not as affected as you speak? For sure, joseph, I am too devastated, I'm caught in this web of a painful parental matrimonial intrigues between mom and dad.

As I speak, do you know my mom have been away from home for the past two months without caring a hoot about what happens in her home? I know my dad is fed-up but he is still holding on to the false hope of his undying love for a loveless mother I know I have. And in all, I sincerely love both my parents, no matter how bad this looks. Joseph, I am lost in this love story that is truly only understood by those who share it--- my parents.

Looking worried and confused, joseph could not help seeing the emptiness and heaviness in those eyes and heart of his friend. The only problem he have is not knowing the right words or advice to give to her in this delicate situation. He must be careful to choose his words right, so as not to futher hurt her tender heart which is bruised from family traumas'. Well, April, I pray God to intervene in whatever problem there is between your parents. I will be praying for each of them night and day, I promise. But can you promise to get yourself out of this dangerous adult web? You know I do not want you to look sad or feel sad my friend, I only want the best grades for us, tell you what, do you think you can take your mind off their problem and come with me to the movies tonight?

Somehow, joseph, I will try, I do want to take my mind off all this indeed, but I honestly pity my father. He is too traditional with his belief in love, family and respect for women to a large extent and I think my dad is too weak a man to handle my mother. My mother is the fire, while he is the ice in this marriage." Do not say that of your dad, I am sure your father knows what he is doing, he alone knows what he wants. He could decide to talk things over with his wife whenever she returns. 'Ha, ha! Laughing hysterically at joseph's last words,'' whenever she returns indeed! My mother couldn't care less if my dad is emotionally wrecked or not. She doesn't care if dad is deprived of her love and attention not to talk of dedicating her time for him whom she married. Well, I pray God to stand by dad to give him the strength to continue in this painful humiliating marriage to my mother. 'Ok, I say AMEN!! To that prayer for you, can we now go? Still holding hands as they walk back to class.

Back in the hotel room in Kenya, Dean could not resist missing out on this lifelong opportunity. He walked slowly to carol in the balcony of her hotel suit, ''carol, please do understand how I feel right now, I'm sure you know I have great respect for you, I'm also sure you know where I stand in my solicited relationship with you, that is if ever you oblige this aching, hungry heart of a man, truly in love with a forbidden fruit as it is.

But, I am willing to taste of this poison if only to die by it. In your arms only do I wish to die like a slave of your love? Carol, I wish today to die by the poison of your love''. He kneel down in front of her, holding her sweaty hands in his, tears welled up in his eyes, he gently reach out to her heart from his with the strong emotional music his heart and eyes are playing inside this room.

Not knowing how to respond or what to do, carol can see deep inside the heart of this man kneeling, holding her hands. The burning desires of love flowing from his hungry hands, keeping her warm and protected in his arms like never before. But, is this really what she wants, could this be the only remedy towards solving this nagging headache that Mr. Kanga's approval has become? That and many more questions keep turning in her melting heart. She have not for long seen herself faced with this sexual urge and temptation from a man for a very long time. Fascinated as she is, she will not bring her weakness to show before this man. This is a critical moment for her to do what is right before God and man. But to her, it is a moment to behold in her minds eyes for a longtime to come.

Whatan irony! What will happen if she resist this dangerous love adventure? What will be the outcome of her accepting or refusing this poisonous love portion? What will be the result of allowing herself to get drunk in this darkness, weakness of the flesh against the desires of this heart? A heart longing to be the woman that she is instead of this "man" she pretends to be before the entire world? Well, for a moment, she drifted in the idea to let Dean have his way. Even when she knew it could end up damaging her marriage and reputation. Yes, her marriage, does it still really exist? Has she really been a good wife and mother to her family? These questions she ask in her feeble mind forgetting for a while the man who is sweeping her little frame off the floor to her massive bed in the hotel room, caressing her body, plastering her whole warm naked body with hot kisses from a sexually desperate Casanova like him, she responded by pretending to shut her eyes.

For a while, lust in the passion of the moment, helplessly, thoughtlessly of the implications there after, for sure, Dean capitalized on the weaknesses of this brief second to deflate her ego, defenselessly, he ravishingly devoured her like a hungry lion tearing up a life goat for dinner in his cage!

He squeezed her succulent breast, kissing passionately with his lips stroking her harden pointed nipples and his strong hands running through the back of her neck, down to her long black hair. At this point, she surrendered completely to the touch of his magic fingers, working hungrily through her naked body.

Carol let go of herself! She felt good for a moment in the euphoria of the deep passion, probably because she have not had it this good for a long time with her husband Richard. This is because she deliberately did not want it to happen between them, haven lost every feeling of love for her husband a long time ago, her body could not resist Dean's sexual touch.

Dean is not one that misses a target, digging deeper into her body, he realized for the first time that this "big fish' (carol) is different for him. He realized that he felt different holding this woman in his arms body to body naked! A feeling that he thought was dead in him. How could this be happening to me? I 'm a play boy, feelings or love is not part of me. What is going on with me? I'm never back to a house hole, after conquering its exquisite designs of its entire triangular section of a woman's body!

For him, going down the same road twice with a woman is a taboo, he always strikes once, leave his mark and run. But with carol, he knew that he certainly will like to break this rule, he would like to pass this road again, and again if possible to leave a mark and signature in her triangle section which could be traced back to him for life. He made love to her like never before in his life with any woman. She too responded so well to her amazement, she could not believe she is the same wife of Richard, mother of children, the strong powerful diplomat who must be obeyed by all. She was shaking under the drunkenness of this sweet love making with Dean, forgetting the person she is. This is surely one big phase in her life that will never go away so easily with the shutting of her eyes.

After satisfying each other sexually, they both slept off beside each other on the massive bed that bore the mark and history of this deadly secret. The alarm clock rang out angrily as though condemning the act that has just taken place before it from the bed side table waking carol up from what she thought to be a wet dream. She looked casually at a naked male body by her side and wondered who it was. But her glance returned back to the man on the bed realizing the figure it was, sleeping peacefully like a baby under her bed sheets face down, she thought for a while she was missing something and sprang up forcefully from her bed. Quickly covering her naked body with one of the sheets on the floor which is littered with a tell-tale of last night's event, she rushed to the bath room first to see if there is anything to awaken her suspicion that it was real something happened between her and the figure lying on her bed naked.

Inside the toilet bowl was three unflushed used condoms and pieces of used tissue papers on the floor of the marble tiled room. She opened her mouth, no words could be heard, and her eyes wide open in disbelief, so ashamed and more confused, she rushed back from the bath room to the bed room to wake up the man to be sure who he is and her worst night mare confirmed! "get up, hi, get up from my bed. Wake up" shaking and pulling violently at him. Dean, you? How did you get on my bed? What happen between us, did you spend the night here with me? What happen? Don't tell me we did it, please don't confirm that! Oh' my God, what have I done? I'm finished! My reputation and marriage is finished, you slept with me Dean, and you did it! Calm down please, let me explain, it's not what you think, we did it, not I doing it. I couldn't have done it without your help. Don't say it like that please. You are different, believe me. No, get out of my room now! Seeing her reaction with such rage, he quickly dressed up without having the time to button his shirt and he left. He knew for sure this is one hell of a day for him, but in all, mission accomplished, the satisfaction he got from holding her sweet, naked succulent body in his arms is enough for him to accept any insult or ranting from this woman.

There and then, he resolved within himself to stand and face whatever happens after now in this new chapter of his adventurous life. Resolving never to retreat or surrender to her or any other intimidation and obstacles that might come his way, he will go any length to prove his love for her sincerely.

This is the first woman in Deans' life that he has ever felt anything for genuinely in a bid to conquer her ego. He got his heart conquered by her instead! Both of them knew something has changed in their entire lives. For carol, how can she face her husband or children when they find out what happened in this quiet Kenya hotel room? If truly this desire inside her is nothing to worry about, can she let go the weaknesses of the flesh whenever again she runs into this guy? She knows that the weakness of the flesh is not an easy thing to give up for most people when it comes.

The end of the road this seems to be for everything she holds dear, deep down in her heart, she knew something has been awaken in her, a demon of sort has been awaken in her by Dean! This to her could be the proverbial straw that breaks the camel's back! Only time to tell.

Dean got home from the hotel and decided to spend the remaining part of the day rummaging in his mind the events of the previous night. He sat down alone in the basement of his luxury apartment in an up brow area of the city, the sensation from the satisfaction he got from the sexual encounter with carol, running through his body like cold water, once again, there is no doubt whatsoever, that this is it at last for this international play-boy.

The play- boy is finally in love with the most unusual of women, in love with the biggest poison of our time. How did I get to this road with love? I should have known she was trouble for my heart right from the onset, he said aloud. Well, I can't' fight this no more, maybe it is time I truly become responsible for once in my life when it comes to women. But, will this woman continuously allow me drink from her triangular poisonous zone? With this cup of wine in-between my two legs, I'm sure like to drink from her poisonous triangular zone, if she allows me forever. I have entangled my restless wondering soul in a dangerous web of sexual poisonous intrigues of life. How do I face her husband? What do I tell her children? And the world, how do I face you? How do they come into all this? My God, help this helpless man, who finds his first real love in the passion of hot poison. It's been a week ever since he stepped out of his house, he had spent the better part of the week thinking of carol, without knowing what next to do. Dean decided it was time once again, to face his fears rather than hide away in the shadow of the unknown.

After a warm hot bath in the shower, he got dressed and decided it was time to visit carol in the hotel to see what her next reaction would be. Since their last encounter, carol have been out of communication with the world, soaking herself in regrets and uncertainty of what lies ahead in this unholy encounter with Dean. He on his part, in between the week, tried severally to reach her on phone without luck. A quick dash to her hotel by me will not hurt a fly, he thought to himself, it was the only option left since he wouldn't want anybody to know what happened between them.

Inside in the hotel lobby just by the elevator entrance to the top floor, he saw the extroverted nosy front door desk lady, smiling at him seductively,' good morning sir, hi there, how are you doing today? Good to see you sir, we thought you went out of town as usual sir? Not really, I 'have been very busy lately.

Your friend upstairs left two nights ago sir. Who? The lady you were with last week, the diplomat lady from New York City, Mrs. Richard Whiteman. Oh, I see. He stood abruptly for a while, not knowing if to inquire more from this nosy person or pretend as if nothing serious between them. I thought you were going up to her suit sir that is why I felt I should let you know she is gone. Ok, well, not quiet, I just came by as usual to see some other person, thanks anyway, I should be on my way now, thank you for the information once again.

Always my pleasure sir, smiling. He walked disappointedly back into the cold morning breeze, what is going to happen now that she is gone? He can only hope and pray to find her back again to know if this feeling inside is mutual. But why did she leave suddenly, how did she go with Mr. Kanga? Did she finally get the contract from this man for her country? What happen, did she leave because of what happened between them? Could she be running away from the fact that she too is in love with him? These are questions only carol Richard Whiteman (JR) can answer! Dean desperately need answers to know what she feels for him and what happened with her business deal with kanga. Later that afternoon, he stopped over at kanga's office to see if he could get any clue as to what became of carol's business deal with him. Hello grace, hello sir, quiet sometime, what brings you here today sir? She knew Dean rarely visits his friend and her boss, Mr. Kanga often. Well, I just came by to see how you all are doing, is Mr. Kanga in the office? Yes sir, but are you on appointment? No, but I'm sure he will be happy to know I'm here.

You know how close we are, just mention to him that I am here please. Ok, give me a minute. She smartly worked to the oak office to announce to her boss his presence. On his part, kanga has been on the lookout for his friend Dean, good in helping kanga settle up in the area where he is deficient in the handling of international business trades, at this point, he needed him to help sort out his problem with a rival company over tax matters.

Dean is very useful in this regard, he has been an intermediary for people who need his services, companies and organizations to settle and arrange deals. Through each successful deals or businesses arranged, he gets substantial amount of money from the deals to maintain his expensive play boy life style.

This time, it was like using one stone to kill two birds, the big oak door opened, there standing behind the framed wooden desk with glass top was the massive body of the African man who looks and behaves more like the late Idi -Amine of Uganda, in all majesty and glory. Mr. Kanga is a big man, he commands both respect and fear from the local folks in his community. But he can be as gentle as a dove whenever he wants and as deadly as a serpent most times. He is very mindful of his dealings with people, and still prefers to apply his traditional African way of doing things. He puts that first before any other thing.

Seeing Dean that afternoon, kanga was over the moon with excitement because he could finally lay to rest once and for all, the rival business deals to his advantage with his help. He smiled grimly, stretched out his big hand towards Dean for a hand shake' hello my friend, good to see you, please have a sit, I have been looking for you all these while, where have you been? Thank god I finally found you. What can we do for each other today? Hope you have not fallen into trouble with any of you numerous women again? Dean smiled broadly and settled down on the sofa beside the oak table in the well-furnished office. The office is adorned with various artifacts, samples and real, dry heads of various animals and African art works from different artists, added to the beauty of this office. Responding, Dean defended himself saying, no, no, I just was in your neighborhood and decided to stop by to see you. Did I do wrong to come see my friend? With a broad smile on his face, kanga retorted back, of course not my friend, I'm always delighted to have you around.

Chapter 4

Dean noticed that kanga was really too eager to tell him something, unknown to kanga, he also was in a hurry to ask about carol, who blinks first? He felt he should be the first because of his hunger for information for carol. He desperately wants to know about her. What do I offer you friend? Oh, I just take ice water please, it's still too early to hit the bottle in an office, and you know my style. Kanga offered him a glass of ice cold water. Sipping from his glass of water slowly and impatiently, dean decided to break the silence, so, how is business with the chambers these days? I hope you have great opportunity to expand your business this time around to foreign countries?

Do you have any business dealings or contract recently, any offer for New York this year? New York is one of the new prospects we have, but I have a problem with their representative. Dean swiftly move to the other side on the sofa hearing the news, he readjusted his seating position again as kanga mentioned the word 'representative' he knew who he was referring to and that to him was the jackpot information he has been looking for.

It was like an easy way out for him in his squest for carol and if possible, this will help him get to the contract for carol and could win him her heart, considering how important this was for her. If he can get kanga to give New York this contract, that is the big deal for him and carol to see each other again he thought. Now, he is more convinced she never finished the business with Mr. Kanga as expected, this was what brought her to Kenya and to him in the first instance he felt he was responsible to still make this possible, since it was the link that brought them together in finding his true love in carol.

Tell me Kanga, what is the problem you are having with the New York representative? Maybe I can be of help here. Ok, that would be a relief, that woman is unbelievable, but I admire her intelligence, I guess that is the only thing going for her. I wonder what type of man that tolerate such a woman? She is so unbearable and very abusive for my type of person, I can't stand her for a second longer like that! Can you believe she did not turn up for our appointment last week after several last minute cancellations? Well, I guess she too got pissed with my over bearing African attitudes. Obviously, two captains cannot be in this ship. Everything kanga said about carol made Dean even love her more, each condemnation is like adding more love portion (poison?) to his over bloated love adrenaline. He smiled, shake his head tilted to the left of his shoulder like the African male red necked lizard, (the Agama lizard) wooing the female for sex.

He remembered how his lips in her mouth, felt sweet sensation which transmitted to every other part of his body the moment they locked lips in a passionate kiss. How she responded by grabbing her tongue in his mouth and hungrily kissed away in to the innocence of the night.

Lost in the hot ecstasy of love, the sweet sensation still lingers in his heart, it is a testimony of the night shared in true hot romance by both. Dean, are you ok? Yes, I see in your eyes, lost in its only world, telling its own story. Did I say anything to betray that emotions? Yes my friend, you only see in someone lost in passion that type of sudden glow you have. Dean smiled, proudly, he understood what Mr. Kanga meant, if only kanga can see what picture is going through his mind, he said as they spoke, he was only thinking of business, I was only lost in my business worries, you know how it goes these days, you know I want you to tell me about this woman and the new York deal.

Did their representative just disappear or what? I was told she fell sick and had to go back to her country, can you believe that? Mr. Kanga asked. Well, what do you make of that? Me? Yes, you, what do you think about that woman standing me up? I don't think she deliberately did that, maybe she is really sick. But what are you going to do about that? I sincerely do not know. I'm willing to go to New York for you my friend and get that woman make this deal. I'm ready to get you that deal kanga." I trust they will do a good job with their technological advancement in world economy, I can help.

Dean, all she needed to do was to humble herself, drop those nasty character and simply ask me. Would you have given her the deal for her country kanga? Sure Dean, I would have given her the juicy deal right away! Excited as Dean was, he did not want his friend kanga to know what great news he had just given him. The opening he has been waiting for is finally here. He had to take this opportunity now or miss it forever, he said." Can I ask you something? Sure, anything Dean." Can you be kind to let me have every information you have of this woman in New York and let me bring her to you so that we can get this deal over with? Both of your country need each other, pride should not deprive your people of this good opportunity for open doors in world economy.

I will ask my secretary, Madam Grace to make every information available for you as soon as possible right. Back in his hay days, Dean would not expect to be the one seeking desperately for a woman's address, rather the opposite was the case while he hides from them as much as he could. Women always beg him for his numbers and contact information after each encounter with him. But with this woman, carol, the reverse is surely the case for Dean.

After leaving kanga's office, he went straight home to pack his suit case for his journey to New York, this trip for him is a big deal because he will see carol and determine whether they both have a chance together. He would find out if he will be rejected or accepted by the woman he has fallen in love with. The only fear at the back of his mind is--- what lies ahead, will she refuse my love? Rejection is, never an option or a familiar terrain for him to walk.

All his life, no woman has ever rejected him but one way or the other, he prepared his mind for the worst as he leaves to see this woman who has stolen his heart for real. The early morning sun was just rising in the sky when Dean entered his car for the airport, on his way driving through the streets, he wondered how beautifully God created the things of this world. The trees were full of beautiful green fresh leaves, birds singing, going about their daily routine of flying half the world and back. He saw how amazing the ocean tide swayed from one point to the other with different people surfing, relaxing and enjoying this free gift of nature.

Behind him was an open field which reminded him of his days in his native home of Tennessee. As a kid, he will go out of his parents' ranch to the football field close to his school to play football with other kids. After that, he returns home to eat dinner prepared by his mother who cared most for the family, Dean had a blissful family up bringing from a decent average family in Tennessee. He never had the opportunity as most teenager to experiment with sex or women, he was too protected by his mother's love and words of the bible read from mamas' lips to do anything unbecoming. He always cherishes those moments of his life when he try's comparing it to what he grew up to become, sometimes, he sees himself as a bird who just escape from the cage where it was for a century.

The breeze from the side of the car mirror, cascading his face elegantly, he used his left hand to remove some part of his hair flying all over his handsome face. He sees all this as part of the beauty of the city he lives.

At the airport, his flight was a little delayed due to the storm the previous night, he finally boarded few minutes later and enjoyed his flight to new York, he was sleeping, dreaming about meeting carol again all through the flight. Carol could not imagine herself, sleeping so long with all her clothes on.

Wondering where precisely she was, she knew that life can never be the same again for her. Nothing looked the same any more, for a while, it was the gentle footsteps and tapings on the door that awaken her from this slumber to the reality before her.

The true existence of a family so rejected, abandoned and deeply unappreciated by her, this is a family that needs to be respected, protected, loved and adored by her because they have been there for her. A family she herself have loved to be a part of, a family which she created with a loving man by her side all the way. She lay back on the bed for a while, flashes of the good old days with her husband Richard Whiteman (JR), she wondered why she allowed that to die, why? Why?? God, why? What went wrong in this marriage? I neglected my family with my own hands, I have never been there for them, sobbing, and carol knew she has reached a breaking point in her life. Streams of tears rolled down her check, she wept profusely on the bed, without any further doubt, there comes a time in the affairs of men, when conscience, which is an open wound, becomes the only mirror we use to see ourselves. It is the only thing that now plays a prominent role for us in the quiet moments of our troubled lives.

She knew there and then that, if indeed conscience is an open wound as they say, and if indeed she has one, then it is only the bitter truth that she is a failure to herself and family no matter how bitter, that can heal her marriage. The big problem is-----CAN SHE REJECT OR RESIST DEAN WHEN SHE COMES FACE TO FACE WITH HIM AGAIN? This is the question which only she can answer, still in that mood, she got off from the bed, took her bath and decided to face life as it comes. Back in the posh apartment living room, her husband and kids were already having breakfast. She arrived home the previous night unnoticed and uncaring. Suddenly after about two (2) months of impromptu travel absence from the family, carol didn't know what to do.

Richard and the children have been living their lives without her, they know she have no apology or sorry for anyone of them. She rules and have no explanation to offer her husband or the children after such long absenceses from home, she has automatically assumed the headship of the family in that house much to the charging of her children.

But unknown to her, she has long destroyed the good home God gave her with her own hands, gradually, Richard turned his head to see who was coming out of the other room. From the corner of his eyes, he saw his wife stagger out of the door, he did not know what to do or how to react to what he was seeing, whatever he saw and felt was first hidden from the children in the dining table. The only thing he knew, was that he was just neutral to his wife's sudden appearance from the moon as it were to him.

It has been her routine to come into the house whenever and go whenever without a word of her movement to anyone. And whenever she comes back, she always end up sleeping in the opposite room to their bedroom for reasons best known to her. This attitude to Richard is the sign of a marriage that has fallen down, regretfully which is the marriage he finds himself engulfed with from the woman he loves so much.

Words alone is not enough to express what pain he is going through inside, sometimes in a man's life, the pain is only known to the man who wears no shoes in the rain. He alone knows what it feels like to be drenched in the rain in a cold winter night without shoes, clothes or shelter! Because of his love for his late mother and the promise made to the dead, he has no choice for now than to keep soaking in this bitterness of love as it is-but for how long can this go on like this? Only he and time will tell.

Coming back to reality from all his thoughts, Richard looked up to his children to announce the arrival of their mother. Your mother is home, have you guys seen her? There is no doubt that the children are not too excited to hear the news, they are not even excited to see her because they are so used to her absenteeism. She is always the one that cares for herself as from the beginning of the marriage. That is how she wished it to be. As ever, April was the first to speak, Sam just got up and walked out the front door to school without a single word for her.

He has always been that way ever since he was born. Like his father, he hates anything that will disturb his life emotionally or otherwise, he just can't stand it. Although, he is a very sensitive young man with great potentials for life, he has a very strong sense of character to hold his own as a young man, "daddy, she is your wife, I hope you find the courage this time to tell her what your truly feel? Let her know the kind of wife she is to you and help us ask her the example of a mother she is to me in particular, I sure will like to know her response since she is highly intelligent.

It is time you come out of the shell daddy, you are in horror, I see you go through all this pain and I wonder what a principled father you are for love? All these years daddy, you have been holding on and you still hold on for the sake of love and promise to your mother? She walked up to him, put her hand on his shoulder squeezing it softly as tenderly as possible, hugging him like she is about losing him and lay her head on his shoulders before leaving for school that day without saying hello or welcome back home to a mother she might not see by the time she comes back home from school.

Richard Whiteman (JR) remained in that sitting position for a while with his head down on the table, he wept bitterly from the heart like never before. For him it was a wakeup call for action from his daughter whom he never believed could be so matured in words and action, he wept for two main reasons, one she reminded him again of his mother's tender love and care which brought him to this point of mare stupidity for his wife and second, he realized that day that his daughter considers him a weakling in the marriage.

This to him, is totally unacceptable. But which way out Richard? Where is your escape? This is what his late mother would have said to him at this point in time with that final gentle stroke and hug from her, he thought that it is truly time to seat down and have a talk with his wife carol, after all, she is still my wife, I married her, he thought to himself to boost his moral.

In actual sense of it, Richard has been afraid for a while to talk with carol, he has been so emotionally traumatized to the extent of losing his self-esteem before her. This fear of the unknown is the beginning of wisdom for Richard and the worth of a promise made to his late mother is all crashing down his life before his very eye, that promise is killing him gradually.

Knowing for sure the woman he married, he thought it wise to leave all talks for the evening time when the children will be home. He felt in the quiet of the night, he would wake her up if she allows him sleep with her for that night, it will be an opportunity for this all important talk. Carol finally emerged from the bedroom with her office brief case and pocket book in hand ready to go.

Hi, I came in late last night, I felt it wasn't necessary to wake you guys up, so I went straight to bed. Of course, I was tired and weak from an exhaustive journey so I didn't want to wake you up, I slept in the spare room. Where are the children? They have gone to school i suppose? She looked at her husband casually, no kiss, no hug, no sorry or I miss you all these while. Only a silly casual look a master gives to his house maid, which was all Richard got from his wife. She stood by the door, sipping from her coffee cup, without remorse or guilt, facing her husband whose miserability is very obvious by now and turned towards the outside door as she made for her car hurriedly.

At this stage, Richard rushed after her and requested for a few minutes of her time. Hi, can we talk please? I believe you owe us a lot of explanation, I mean I'm still your husband and you are still the mother of my children. Can you ever have time for this family? I don't know what to tell you, but if this home is crumbling, if you are a problem or I the problem, I have a right to know why? You are a problem to me and the children carol.

For a moment, she stepped back and walked quietly into the house with Richard, stood still for a moment starring coldly at her husband with wide open eyes and said, is that you talking Richard or I didn't hear right? Well, since when did you start questioning my authority in this house? Do I look stupid or foolish to you? Look, I don't care what you or the children think and feel, I have my life and my carrier ahead of me. But don't you know I did you favors to have married and have this children for you? You should be thankful at least for that! You all should be thanking me enough for the rest of your miserable lives! She hissed like a dangerous viper snake and walked right pass Richard to her car outside.

Ha! Richard could not believe what he has just heard from his wife. He knew it was a bad situation, but he never realized it was this bad. Hold it right there woman! If I may ask, what sort of favor did you do for us? Oh, oh, you mean you don't yet see it? Well, I did you a favor by marrying you and having kids for you, period! I should have chosen to abort these pregnancies if I like, but you all should thank god I was in good mood the day I took in and gave birth to them for you. Today, they are your legal advisers who conspire with you against me their mother, I don't blame you all.

She entered her car and drove off for about a mile to her office, she broke down in tears for reasons she cannot even explain. Something in her is yearning for a change, but the other side of her is still hungry for war with whoever.

This has been a conflict in her battles with lives wrong and right. Her conscience is judging her, telling her she is wrong by her hurting behavior to her family, but the person she is will never allow her accept this much fact before her husband, talk less of the world, to her acceptance is a sign of weakness. Should I go back to Richard and apologize? Do I go to my children's school, individually to do the same? She thought for the family sake, it would have been better to make peace for all, but this pride will not let her be the mother and wife she is' I must remain strong, I mustn't show any sign of weakness to this wicked world, but I must keep fighting this as much as I can.

She said to herself that this family has been destroyed by her, especially her husband Richard. Is it the ring that makes the home or the wearers of the ring's attitude that builds the home? Well, to her, she ask this question to no one in particular but herself in thoughts at that time. I know it is the actions and in actions of the people that wears the ring at any point in time that makes a marriage work or fail. This is a fact I know so well, but cannot accept in my own life. What an irony of life! Carol lay all the blame on her parents.

She resented them for the kind of upbringing she had and wondered if things could have been different for her if she was not their daughter. She knew she married one of the best of men in the person of Richard Whiteman (JR), but quickly changed her thought saying, there was no space for regret in her heart for now. She wiped the tears off her face with the back of her hand as she approached the official car park in her 6th floor office building. Good morning Mrs. Whiteman, good to see you back on your desk, we all miss your presence here. Her personal staff in her office know how to make her feel important, they all know that whenever she is around in the office after such long absence from duty, the office becomes hellish for them all.

She will scream, yell, cause and swear for whoever is unfortunate enough to fall in to her trap. In fact, her direct staff always pray for her to travel long time away from office for official reasons than be around the office most of the time. This gives them liberty and comfort for a while until she returns. What is good about this morning that you all are smiling about? Anyway, I thank you for doing nothing in my absence other than gossip all day, I take that as a very warm welcome, can we all now get back to work? It is a beautiful Monday morning, the sun is up and the sky is bright, so, move it people! This is no surprise at all to them, rather, it is a familiar statement which they are used to. Everyone exchanged quick glances, making faces of, here comes trouble again' 'before they all left for their various desk. She quickly perused through the bulky files on her desk half hazard, her mind going back and from the encounter of the day with Richard.

Another part of it wonders back and from the event in Kenya with the sexual passion she enjoyed with Dean. Even though she refuses to accept it to herself, she knew she wanted more of that action again. She was not truly ready to work on files or deal with anybody that day, her mind was not at its best at all. She passed some of it to the Ambassador for further action." Tell the Ambassador I'm off for launch. Yes madam.

Her secretary, Kate is a very serious minded workaholic, too serious and sometimes too religious. She is the only secretary who agreed to work with carol and the only one who has stayed most with her, this some say is because of her religion that she has managed to accept Carol this long. No one in that office, both men and women, high or low ever agrees to work under her. She is known all over the mission building and across as a very irritating person to have any meaningful talk with, if those that deal with her at all have an alternative, they will not deal with her not even with a long pole!

But as time passed, since her return, her only fear is what to tell the Ambassador concerning the Kenya deal. The contract meant everything for her carrier and her country, but this is truly a trying first time she failed to get what she wants. It is the first time, despite her bad character, that she has been unfaithful to her husband, Richard. Well, there must always be a first time in everything she thought," I must get this over with, I must take Dean off my mind and my head to stay sane, for the better part of her launch break, the thought of going back to Kenya to get back the deal occupied her mind.

Rather than thinking of building back her family, she chose instead to think of her carrier as always. Nothing comes between her and her carrier! Drifting between reality and illusion, she suddenly saw a shadow figure that flashed through her table quickly from across the other side of the restaurant. No! It's not what I think it is, I must be tired from my stress that cannot be him, Dean is in Kenya, he does not even know where I work, after all, I did not give him any contact information about me. How can he find me? How can he find me like that? She paid for her launch and walked across back to the office.

As she stepped into the office, Kate approached her with an envelope, with a certain phone number from a certain man who came earlier on looking for her without an appointment. The man said that she should tell her to call the number whenever she comes or Kate should call him whenever she is around from launch break. As soon as carol stepped into her office from her launch break, she handed her the envelope with the number from the stranger who came earlier on to see her, she delivered his message as religiously as possible to her boss.

Who did you say he was? He didn't say his name, but he said if you call that number, you will surely know him. That for Carol, was an insult, thinking aloud, who the hell does he think he is? The Prince of Wales or the President of America? Look here, I am not in the mood for nonsense today, you better do your job well or you lose it, she yelled at her secretary as she tucked the envelope beside her desk and settle down to work without looking inside to see or know who or where the person came from or what his purpose was.

Typical of her, Kate thought to herself and walked back to settle down to work. Unknown to Carol, that envelope she threw away in the trash and the simple single call she refused to make, lies the answer she needs for her carrier right now. It is the key to solving her carrier problem with Mr. Kanga, it could also be the icing on the cake for a new romance in her life---but will history repeat itself if and only when she fails herself again with Dean? As for Dean, he arrived New York the previous night with high expectations, he went straight to the hotel before making contact with one of his numerous contact aids. He has a lot of younger men who look up to him as a role model that he sends as informant for certain special information's on people wherever he goes. He gives them money and gift to their satisfaction to do any of his biddings, no matter how bad it looks. This particular guy in New York is only known as 'killer', they code name him killer because he has no milk of human kindness as long as money is involved. He can do anything for anybody for money without looking back, but if you fail to meet up with his payment, he turns against the person. Whichever way, killer is a time bomb waiting to explode for the world of money and Dean thought it wise to use him for this mission to spy on carol and give him all information necessary.

He came back with all the details as requested by Dean and made sure that he personally briefed Dean, he even wished to accompany Dean for extra cash whenever he wants him to. Killer spied on Richard and the children for a period of time before Dean's arrival, he has a similar job six months ago when one business man from Russia ask him to feed him details on carol. She had been seen with the Russian millionaire some time ago when the guy visited the Ambassador who is a family friend of his. At that occasion, the ambassador requested carol to help make his friend comfortable during his two weeks stay in New York and she was seen getting close to the guy who was madly in love with her intelligence, but for carol, she knew what could happen with this Russian if she ever forget she is married.

The guy was ready to take a step further with her if she give him the green light and it was at that point of the man's life that he employed the services of killer to know more about this woman, carol. Unfortunately, that story did not end well because as usual, her bad manners during one of their outing, put off the Russian interest in her, he was thinking then of bringing carol into his business interest in the state. He wanted to use her secure more power in the international business world with her position and intelligence. The next morning, Dean arrived carol's office which was just an hour drive from the hotel he lodged, he came armed with the contract approval letter from Mr. Kanga for carol, something she has been looking forward to have in her hands all these while. He came not only to give carol this good news, but to also know what she feels for him and ask for her love face to face. He got to the elevator, ascended to the sixth floor where carol's office is, as soon as the elevator door opened in the sixth floor, he stepped out to the scent of lavender perfume, a familiar scent he associates carol with.

Lavender is one of her favorite flower and perfume. The scent washed through his nostril, it brought back nostalgic memories of that silent night when carol won his heart as they made passionate love in that hotel room back in Kenya. It was the same kind of scent he perceived at the alley way that bright sunny morning when he first met her in Kenya. Smiling broadly as he walked towards the door on the left of the lobby, he walked through the beautifully decorated lobby before entering into the elegantly furnished office.

Chapter 5

Inside the office, he saw carol's secretary, Kate smiling at him warmly. 'How can I help you sir? HI, I hope l am in the right office? I would like to see Mrs. Carol Richard Whiteman please. You are in the right office sir, are you on appointment? Well, no, is she expecting you sir? I'm not sure, but I am sure she will like to see me. Sorry sir, you can't see her now, but you can drop her a message if you don't mind. Today is not her visiting day, but if it is very important, you could book an appointment. Ok, just help make sure she gets this (handing her an envelope with his name and phone number and the hotel he is staying), tell her to call the number inside that it is urgent, please. Who should I say gave me this? Just tell her to call the number and she will know. Ok, thanks for coming sir.

Dean did not completely leave the office building, he decided to spend some more time watching to see if carol is anywhere around, just for the love of it, he looked forward to seeing her again that day. Never has he ever found himself so hopelessly in true love for a woman before like he is now with her. But with her, he is completely helpless, after about four hours wait around the office area, he finally saw her from a distance without her seeing him, as he followed her behind to the coffee shop across the street, his heart raced fast not knowing what action to take.

The idea of approaching her flashed through his mind for a moment, he felt like jumping on her and planting a passionate kiss on her lips, but he knew that could make him lose her forever. Another idea of not jumping but to call out to her still cross his mind, but he thought otherwise and decided finally to watch her from a distance for now. He knew from her character that if he had allowed his emotions take the better part of him, it would end up in disaster for him. He followed her from a distance to the shop where she had launch, watching her every move, he noticed something different in her, he noticed she was ruffled and looked worried, he could not figure out what it was that looks disturbing to her, but his imagination went wild with various kind of thought.

The most feared of all is his thought that she could turn him down because of what happened between them in Kenya, is she worried because of love or hate for me? he asked no one in particular, the first time he saw her that day outside her office building from across the road where he sat watching was when she came out of the office wearing a sexy sky blue skirt suit with blue matching scarf and shoes, walked fast across the street to the coffee shop where she ordered her launch. That was when Dean decided to quickly make an appearance like a shadow pass from the table she sat close to the outside glass windows, this discision by him was to see if she will recognize him or feel him close to her. Because she was not expecting to see him, even though she was thinking of him at that moment she sat there absent mindedly thinking whether to go back to Kenya and get the contract or not.

She obviously was going through so many emotions at that time, she did not notice even when the solution was right in front of her. For the rest of the day, Dean stayed behind, stalking her until late in the night, he followed her home to her house unnoticed by her, saw her children and husband unnoticed by her and even went as far as talking to carol's son, Sam from his car as he rode pass him on his bike.

The pain in her legs still left her in- capacitated to escape from this bully, never in this life did Eliza ever believed in this moment to come, even when she was is on the dusty floor in the middle of nowhere with her granddaughter, the hope of running from this desert like place is unthinkable. Each hour edges closer to the darkness that craves within her bleeding heart, she thought the only way out is to obey and befriend this bully who seems to be her only way out. But, to this moment, she still could not understand why she and her granddaughter was kidnapped from the mall. All she knew was the car suddenly scratching to a halt beside the bumpy road leading to nowhere in particular for her and the child in her arms.

With nothing to call her own, the stillness of her mind gave rise to the sudden awareness of the distance they drove far from the dusty hut that day. Down the bumpy road of no return the bully drove, inside the truck was the clothes and bag she had on her the day she was kidnapped, all she knew was that this bully could be moving them to another place where he will probably kill them or sell them to another person or whatever he wants to do with them. The least thought in her mind was freedom, she never saw the possibility of this strange man letting them go, certain things just don't seem right with this whole movement with the bully guy whose eyes is death for her. The previous day, she had dreamt of a better ending with a better tomorrow, expecting life to be kind to her after all she had given back to life. As a child, one of her greatest wish was to be the best in whatever she does, even when most events in her life make things difficult for her, she still strives to become a better person for herself.

The worst blow for Eliza was the sudden end to her education which put an end to that dream, today, life has taught her a different lesson, it has taught her the bitter lesson to never trusting again even those who pretend to be close to her who end up hurting her the most in life. Life for her is never a bed of roses, as a child, growing up for her was not easy, she always thought life was beautiful in pictures but the pictures of her life are not beautiful at all to still hold on to that believe. Eliza grew up as a 'tom-boy' girl child the hard way. She was sent away by her people when they discovered she got pregnant by her teacher in her junior high school in Africa, the teacher denied responsibility and never bothered to know what happened to her or the pregnancy, that way, she was exposed to the vagaries of life in a very cruel world by those who should love her. She then wondered in to the vain world and ended up a maid at the hand of a colonial seamstress who taught her the duties of a perfect housewife, growing up to become a decent young lady of the British colonial era. This kind lady who took Eliza in with her pregnancy, tendered to her until she delivered her baby girl in her madam's house.

The child was given away for adoption in a foster home and she never knew what became of that child, until so many years again when fate brought her to meet her lost daughter. That child today is the mother of the granddaughter they kidnapped her with, that is why this incident brought back bad memories to her. After her rejection or banishment from her home, she wondered into the world to survive with the child in her, she then decided to change her name from Ada to Eliza if only to remove the memories of what fate entrust on her. She remembered how her class teacher then. Mr. Kanga came into her life and took her virginity from her, he took her innocence from her without caring to stand by her in the difficult moments of her life.

She cursed the day Mr. Kanga came into her life to ruin it for her, how could she have known that kanga was just out to use her satisfy his lust for beautiful young girls? Here she is today, with a deep scare in her heart and the burden of caring and carrying this shame to the end. Sometimes, she wondered what became of kanga, if he ever remembers her or feels sorry for what he did to her life, unknown to her, kanga lives every day of his life thinking of what became of her and his child, he never stop regretting or blaming himself for not standing up for her and the child. He never knew if she lived or died because the incident back in their village, created a big enmity between both families who were once close friends.

Ada changed her name to Eliza to hide the pain of her past and to forget the humiliation's and rejections of her life, but what she fails to realize, is that, a simple change of name cannot change the heart. You are still the person that you are inside even after the change of name, it does not change your life. She wondered what will happen the day she tells her story to her daughter Joyce. if and when the time comes. Kanga is the biological father of Joyce from Ada. She now changed her name to Eliza. She is the biological mother of Joyce. Joyce is given out for adoption after her birth by the woman who accepted Eliza (Ada) in as her maid and taught her all she knew before she found and married her present husband, Mr. Charles fumes, a wealthy business tycoon and the owner of a popular cement factory in their country.

He is a man of many parts who have no idea of his wife's past at all. Her kidnap was as a result of a business deal between her husband and a rival who desperately needs to get the deal from her husband's company to his own, he felt the only way to put off Eliza's husband was to kidnap his wife and force him to hands off the deal, it worked for them as Charles eventually yielded to their demands and rejected the deal offer from the government under the excuse that his company does not have the capacity to execute the job. Of course, most people knew that was not the case, they know in that country, that he has one of the best, if not the best of all latest standard equipment's to execute any kind of work perfectly.

It was after his announcement as requested by the kidnappers on the state television news that evening that his company has turned down the contract offer for the construction of the ultra-modern city stadium and 145kilometers of roads leading to the new stadium that the rival who now accepted the deal, ordered the bully to let Eliza go. But unknown to Eliza, to her still thinking inside the back of the bully's truck blindfolded with her granddaughter, the only problem she had was her lack of formal education which she craved dangerously for as a young girl, she was so schooled in domestic affairs by the woman who raised her after she wondered from rejection by her people. This gave her an edge over her peers, her beauty in glowing light skin and plump figure which is what most African men wants in a woman made her any man's choice. The average African man wants his woman full and fleshy, they believe that there should be difference between a man and a woman when they lie together, as for the African man, a man should not be looking for his wife on the bed when the light is off. He should be able to feel and touch her beside him on the bed flesh to flesh even when the lights are out because she is full to touch and hold when making love.(Funny, but true).this particular features earned her the love of Charles who saw her first in the house of the Madam that raised her. As for Charles, his international travels and businesses' has never allowed him the opportunity of settling down with any woman, he sees women as opportunistic fellows who are out to ruin a man who is not careful.

His wealth at that time became an obsession for him, it never allowed him to look beyond himself in love, his fears for over educated women and society women is nothing compared with his love for money, but when he saw Eliza in his friend's house, he decided to marry her because she was not only a raw beauty, but a well brought up young lady, dutiful, humble and a good home maker who can give him that home comfort, but he never knew anything of her past or family. Eliza, goes around with a little piece of her past, inside the dirty bag in the truck, she touched and felt the only thing that reminds her of her home, and she found the framed picture of her late father. It was the key to several riddles hanging over the missing picture which holds the key to the wealth her father left for her as a way of making up for his role in sending her away when she needed him most.

He could not stop her mother and other family people from sending her away with the pregnancy because her controlling mother has bullied her father into submission of her authority in the house. In fact, she became the husband in the house, while her late father became the wife, this to her, was one of the reasons that led to her father's early death. When she learnt of her father's death while on exile, she never stopped blaming her mother for her father's death. That faithful evening, she had returned home desolate and dejected from the market, her Madam, Remi, is not a very patient woman when it comes to doing thing's perfectly. She will scream, yell, throw tantrums at you and even cry or hit you when necessary, all to show her displeasure over anything anytime she considers you are not obedient to her teachings. As a caterer herself, it is pertinent for her that every student under her should live above board in whatever they do.

Eliza had a lot on her mind, sometimes she even forgets the slightest of instructions, and it depends on her state of mind at any given time. She had a very rough day already, only to come home to the sad news of her father's demise from just one look on the faces of the crowd under the mango tree in front of her madam's house. That was the last news she had from her own native land before fate settled her in a man's house as a wife and mother of three other children. The woman who brought the news to her madam is one of the lady's she sends on errands to source for her materials for her catering stuff, she uses them sometimes for outdoor catering services. It was during one of such events that the woman saw Eliza, but was quick to recognize her as Ada the girl from her village who got banished by those who should have loved and protected her, ever since, she has been the only link to her roots for her. She it was who manage to bring back a picture of Eliza's dad after his funeral in their village for her. As time pass by, the truck suddenly came to a halt and the bully pulled Eliza and her granddaughter out on the bare floor on the corner of a busy high way and fled.

Eliza managed to open their blind fold and to her surprise, she was now in the midst of people who wondered who she was. Please, where are we? I need help, please give us water to drink, we need to get to the hospital, please, please help us! They quickly put them in a car and took them straight to the general hospital for urgent medical attention. it was at the hospital before she was sedated to sleep that she gave her husband's name and phone number to the doctor who immediately pass the message to Charles. The major concern for Eliza all through her ordeal in the hands of her kidnapper's was the safety of her granddaughter who came to spend the holiday with her newly found grand mama. It took her time to locate her daughter Joyce, the one she had for Mr. Kanga as a young student after a very long time. It was fate that finally brought them to gather again after she was adopted by a white family in the orphanage home where Madam Remi gave her up for adoption after her birth. The couple visited the orphanage home from the united states as part of humanitarian service to third world countries and after hearing the story behind the birth of baby Joyce(Eliza/Ada's child), the couple now decided to adopt and take her abroad as their own child.

The proprietress of the home contacted Madam Remi and constantly up dated her without her informing Eliza. She thought it wise to put her out of the picture so that she can pick up the pieces of her shattered life, it was after Eliza got married to Charles and during one of their holidays together to the united states that they were invited by the mayor of the city they visited for dinner in his house. As a matter of fact, the mayor, jack ford was instantly drawn to Charles and his wife Eliza when he knew they came from Africa. He felt connected to them one way or the other because his wife, Joyce, is an African originally but adopted by an American family where they met in the University of Texas and got married later. It was at their home that Eliza came face to face with her lost child but unknown to her.

During their women conversation, Eliza was drawn to her instantly without knowing why and Joyce ford too was immediately into her own mother without her knowledge. She told Eliza that she was told by her adopted parents that she was adopted from an orphanage home somewhere in Africa when her adopted parents visited Africa for humanitarian services to third world country. She said they told her that her mother was a young school girl who got pregnant by her teacher who denied her and the pregnancy, and as a result, she was rejected and banished by those who should have protected her. And this she said made her biological mother, to wonder into the world of uncertainty. She the Good Samaritan woman who took her into her home as a maid and she gave birth to her under the care of this woman.

She said after her birth, her mother's mentor now decided to give her away for adoption in the orphanage home and as fate would have it for her, it coincided with the arrival of her foster parents who gave her a new life and new identity. To her, that was a touching thing and so heart breaking for anyone to go through, Eliza could not hold back tears rolling down her check like tap water flowing freely. Both women were crying at this point, drawn to each other's world, feeling the pain in their blood for each other. Joyce, I know what that means, I have walked that road in my own life too. I'm really sorry to hear your sad story. I feel closer to you than you can imagine but I pray and believe if it is your desire, that the good Lord bring you to know your true mother.

The poor woman, whoever she is, must have gone through hell". She moved closer to Joyce and put her arms around her as they both sob on each other's shoulders. It was the laughter of Charles her husband jack ford, Joyce's husband that brought both women back to reality. Are you women having a great time together? Ford ask when he sat close to his wife on the sofa in the left corner of the massive building. They sure are doing well for themselves, with their two lovely children, Jim and Jill, the ford family is a role model for many in that city. I would like both of you to visit us again anytime you are in the country and whenever I visit Africa, I will certainly like to see you again. They finally exchanged addresses and phone numbers as they bid each other goodnight. All through their 1hour drive back to their hotel, Eliza was as cold as the sea, she hardly replied Charles conversations or comments, all her mind and thought was racing through the story Joyce just told her about herself. Can she possibly be my lost child? Is she my blood? Why do I have this feeling strongly inside that she is the one? But madam Remi told me that the orphanage home proprietress is dead and the home no longer exist, how come now this part of me is still racing back after 24years? I need to go back to see Madam Remi as soon as I get back to Nigeria.

She is the only one that can solve the riddle with Mrs. Joyce jack ford and me, yes, I must speak to her. As soon as they got back to Africa, Eliza took the next available flight out of state to delta state in Nigeria where Madam Remi retired to, arrived Nigeria the previous night and drove to a place called coco town where she met again with her mentor. "I have been wondering what happened to my first child, I don't know if she is alive or dead madam, but I know somewhere in my heart, that the good lord will and has kept her safe for me all these years. Did you say the old woman who ran that orphanage home where we gave her up for adoption is dead? Why are you bringing back that sad story of your life? You have moved on pass that darkness in your life, see how well god has blessed you. For me, I think god has compensated you for all the troubles you went through in your life back in Kenya. Why are you now trying to bring back a dead horse in your life? We humans, sometimes we are ungrateful to our creator and too greedy for ourselves. Let this past go, please. Well, as much as I respect you, this can never go away from my life, she was my first blood, the child that defined my destiny, the true story and evidence of my hurt from kanga and the once I call my people. Look at me Madam and tell me for truth if that pain is truly gone. Despite all I have now, nothing can take her place in my life. Sobbing out loud. Don't cry my daughter, the truth is, I was told your child was adopted by an America couple who came on humanitarian ground to Africa.

They took her abroad and gave her a new name, the last I had of her, before the death of the orphanage home proprietress, was that her name was "Joyce" and that she graduated from the university of Texas where she met her husband, I know by now she should be a mother of two kids. Eliza's eyes pooped out of its socket on hearing the name Joyce. This is the same name of Mrs. Joyce jack ford, wife of the mayor she met in Texas, United States. Please tell me that is not true, did you say she went to Texas University and now married with two kids? 'Yes, but why all this question? I have found my lost child, Joyce is my daughter, and she is the one, no two ways about this! I knew it! From the moment I saw her, I felt my blood gushing hot inside me, God be praised! Now I know my sufferings are all not in vain. I can die in piece knowing that I found the first missing part of my youth. Where is kanga now? I wish to find him let the humiliation he gave my youth return upon his heads shamefully, Remi, before you left us in Kenya, did your late husband mention anything about kanga's where about? I know he was a man of the law, they are always privilege with vital information.

Madam Remi married a Kenyan where she lived all her life, most people believed she was Kenyan until the death of her husband some years ago did people realized she was not from Kenyan, but a Nigerian born woman who travelled far serving to the needs of the colonial masters of the then. She eventually ended up in Kenya, met fell in love with and married her late husband who was from Kenya. She was not only speechless at this point of Eliza's revelation. She knew deep down in her heart that mother and child would find each other, in fact, she prayed for this day to come. Eliza, putting her frail hands on her as she speak, if you know deep down in your heart that she is your daughter, then go for it. Do not mind what happens after now, just go get your happiness and let that part of you find peace. You have always served me, you are like the daughter I never had if you need my help at any time, just give me a call and I will answer. Even if I'm too old to travel now, I don't mind to help you fulfill this wish for your total happiness. Go my child, bring back home your happiness. Immediately, Eliza went inside her room prepared already for her by madam Remi. She wept and lamented heart achingly reminiscences of her past calling rushing back and from her memories like there was nothing good to smile about. The pains of the past still hurt her like it all just happened yesterday. She woke up very early and left back to base to her husband and children back in Kenya with the heaviness of the past.

Charles noticed at the airport that his wife's eyes were puffy and red, have you been crying? Your eyes are so wet, what happen? I hope Nigeria did not stress you my dear? Not at all, I just want to get home and rest, I hope you will be home early Charles because I would like us to talk. Sure, anything to make my wife comfortable. He kissed her on the lips as she disembark in the front of their palatial home that afternoon. She knew it was time to break the secret to her husband, there was no way she alone could do this on her own without her husband's knowledge at this point. The best alternative is to tell him about her past and let him help he go through it easily. It will be too much for her to handle hiding a secret and letting another exposed with this new discovery of her lost son, but how would she handle the kanga's aspect? Where and who will help her find kanga? These questions keep on in her head as she showered to rest a while before her husband returns, unknown to her, kanga is one of the men her husband deals with.

He is a man he encountered in one of his numerous business meetings some time ago and has remained in touch with for business reasons, whenever they see, they interact as friends, as for Eliza, the other problem troubling her is how to break the news to her daughter, how will she receive the news and how will she accept her? All these questions dwelled with her until the tender touch from her husband, Charles returned her back from the land of worries. I didn't hear you come in Charles, well, I came in few minutes ago, I saw the lights on and I know u were awake. Yes, I could not sleep, was waiting for you to talk, I have a story to tell you and I need you to tell me what you will do if you are in the person's shoes. Does this concern us? Just tell me straight otherwise, I am too tired for other people's story. My husband, it not only concerns us, but it can also divide us if we do not handle it right. Then I must listen, what is bothering my wife? Spite it out, no matter what, I love you too much to leave you. I want you to always remember that my love. No matter what it is, we can and will always overcome. Before you start, let me tell you that I already know what it is. I know that you had a child for someone before I married you, I know that that child was given out for adoption and that you just found out the child is the wife of mayor jack ford in New York. Eliza, but why did you carry this burden alone for so long in your heart? Why did you not trust me enough to tell me these things? Why my love. Why? You should have told me yourself, it would have made this pain lighter for me to bear, oh! My darling, I feel your pain more than you know. He held her close to his chest and for the first time, Charles wept uncontrollably before his wife. Both of them remained in that position weeping on each other's shoulder without caring if and how they will face the tomorrow that is pregnant with so many uncertainties of life.

At this stage, Charles was more than willing to stand by his wife to overcome this trauma, he was determined to help her get the love of her newly found lost daughter and locate the man who is the biological father of the child, unknown to him that he has already found that one. But in her mind, she wondered how her husband got to know this secret she has been hiding for all her life. Her greatest surprise was the receptive way he handled the news, what she was afraid of most has become the simplest matter for her. I know what you must be thinking, when we came back from our trip, I noticed your behavior, you did change a lot to the extent I doubted if you were the same sweet little angel I married.

I didn't know what to do or who to call so, I called the only person I know as your family and the woman who gave you to me in marriage. It was her who narrated to me the true story of your life, I wept then and I'm still weeping now to know that you went through all that alone, I would have still loved you as you are and

I still want to assure you that, nothing has changed between us. I married you for true love and that is even stronger now, tell me, where do we start? She threw herself helplessly on his body and continued weeping like a baby as she speak.

    I'm sorry. I'm sorry my love, forgive me. I did not know what to expect with you. It was stupid of me to think that you will reject me if I tell you that side of me, in fact, I married you to find acceptance and love for once in my life. And I thank you for making me feel loved and protected, you are the only one that has truly treated me like a human being. You make me feel on top of the world, but I need to bring back home my daughter and grandchildren, I want them too to accept me the way you did. Putting up a sweet face, Charles was quick to notice the tender nature of his wife in a different way, he saw the pain in those beautiful eyes of her which caught his fancy many years ago. Don't worry, I promise we will, but do you know anything about the father, like where he is or who he is? I know Mr. Kanga is somewhere here in Kenya. I hear he is now a big shot in the business and commerce sector of this country, but I have never set my eyes on him since I was banished from my home, maybe he is dead or a life, I do not even know now. Wait, what name did you call just now? Did you mention Mr. Kanga? Yes, why? The only important Mr. Kanga I know is the chairman of the Kenya business of commerce and industry, could he be the same sinner we are talking about? I know him. We have met a few times and he sure looks mean to me. if he is, we have solved one big problem my love. Eliza, do we go after your daughter first or look for the father, which do you prefer my love? Just say it and I will do whatever it takes to make it happen. This man, kanga you just talked about Charles, do you know where we can find him here in Kenya? Sure my love I can book an appointment with him tomorrow and we go together to see him. I want you to go with me so that you can identify him. Are you sure you are ready to face him again if he is the same person? I don't know, but that will bring back so many bad memories for me, I just have to prepare myself for the worst. I should be strong enough to do this alone. No, you are not alone, I am with you my love, whatever happens, do not say you are alone anymore.

Now we have each other, I will make the arrangements for that and our journey back to New York as soon as possible if you don't mind. Not at all, the earlier, the better to take this burden off my chest. He kissed her on her lips and exit from the house back to his car. That night heralded a new dawn in Eliza's life, she neither slept nor rested throughout the night all he thought was with her daughter, how she turned out a success out of nothing, how fate took her into the hands of a caring new family and how the child that was rejected by her biological father (Mr. Kanga) turned out to be the wife of a city mayor and a mother of two wonderful kids.

Again, one part of her is afraid to face the man who turned her life upside down, she never knew what his or her reaction would be standing face to face with kanga, what would be her first reaction to this evil man who ruined her life? She thought to herself. Should I jump at him to show how frustrated I was back then, or just ignore him and let him know that I came out of the ashes and shame of his humiliation, rejection and sufferings to becomes somebody in my life? I think it would be better to show him mercy, let him live the rest of his miserable life knowing that myself and the child he rejected came out of those miseries of our twisted lives to make it to the top as best as we could.

Ours is a story of survival in distress and triumph in trials of life, this is a story for him to die regretting all his life when he sees me and my daughter, I think that sight should hunt him forever. And it will be my day of victory, surly, I have laugh last over all my enemies! I will go to him with my head held up high. I will let him know that most times in our lives, it is not the action we take that defines who we are, but the ones we refuse to take when we are supposed to that makes us what we are. I will make him see that in every disgrace of our lives, there is always a grace. I have found my grace in the disgrace of my life with this event of my life. I must learn to forgive him even as I pity him, I pray he finds a place in his heart to forgive himself for what he did to our lives.

Early the next morning, Eliza found herself standing face to face with the worst nightmare of her life! There he stood, glued to the spot, not knowing if to run or hid, he was lost to shame, the shame of a life he thought he ruined forever standing before him in shining glow of victory over defeat! This must be a dream he said, but it was not! This is for real, Eliza and kanga face to face with each other again after the incident that tore them apart In that little village of theirs. Yes, it is I. I am a life and well. This is my husband Charles, Charles, this is he who wanted to ruin my life, kanga, I have forgiven you. I forgave you just last night for all you did to me and our child. Well, life is too short for holding grudges against one and other, I am here to tell you that the child you denied and rejected is the mother of two lovely children in new York and she is the wife of the mayor of a city in the united states, but you rejected us, wrote us off when god did not.

Who can condemn when God has not? Is there a man that can erase what God has written about us? Absolutely not! Because God has found us worthy of his love, I and my daughter have risen above defeat to see this day, you are forgiven. Up until now, kanga could not still utter a word to Eliza. The only words he spoke with his eyes were tears of shame and regret rolling down the cheek of this 6footer man who bears semblance with the late president Idi- Amin Dada of Uganda. No one has ever seen him so weak or fragile to any issue, he has been like an uncrack able rock which cannot be broken or shaken. But he is, standing before his entire staff, crying like a wiped child who has lost his money for food at a local school in the village.

To say the least, everyone was taken aback, seeing this man whose only language with presence sends fear into the heart of both infants and adult alike, cry before the world, this must be serious. The question on the lip of every one is- who is this woman and man visitors that have brought Mr. Kanga to his kneels? Madam Grace, kanga's secretary quickly saved the day, she moved closer to her boss and led him with the important visitors to the inner office and shut the door behind them as she leaves. She knew this was the best she could do to save her master the shame before other people in the office. Back inside, kanga and Eliza were both still crying when Charles decided it was time to break the ice.

His wife was not prepared at that stage to say anything because she was too emotional. Mr. Kanga, I know this is very emotional for both of you, but I want you to know that as a man, I understand what you did. I am not here to judge or lay blame on you, I just want you to know that you have a child whom you need to beg for forgiveness, you two have to put aside your pain or pride and come together to face the child you kanga abandoned. For the first time, kanga found his voice, please Charles, I have wronged your wife and my child, I have lived all these years wondering where they are and what happened to her. You might not fully understand how I regret the bad decision's I made, I was too young and too scared to get up and own up as a man my own mistakes. I crave every day and cry in the loneliness of my heart, that darkness refuse to leave my life, it has tormented me everywhere I go.

But today, I thank god I will be able to put that ghost of my past behind and make a better part of it. The only thing I want you to help me do is beg your wife to first forgive me. I couldn't have imagined to see you like this in my life! All along, you have been close by but I just refuse to see, now, where and how is my daughter? Asking no one in particular, but Charles decided to tell him all he needed to know. Immediately, kanga could not contain his anxiety to go to New York and see his first child. Please allow me to make the arrangements and we travel in the next available flight if that is ok by all? For now, I would like to take my wife home and will get back to you.

She has gone through a lot for one day, thank you for your time and be prepared to see your child. They left kanga's office and went home to prepare. The journey to New York was like travelling from earth to hell for kanga, sitting inside the same airplane with Eliza and Charles can be said to be one of his worst journey experiences in life. They arrived untimed and headed straight to the house were Mrs. Joyce jack ford (their daughter) was already waiting. After Eliza's call the previous day she wondered what it was that could bring her back to New York so soon. As an individual, she is a very sensitive thinker who try so hard to impress people against her comfort, as soon as they came into her home, she knew something big was about to happen. She was wondering who the big-foot like man following behind was. Please to see you again, when you called that you were coming I started wondering why, I hope all is well? Yes, but back in Africa, we have an adage that goes thus" a frog is not seen by the day easily, it is only when there is an emergency that you see a frog by the day" haven said that, we are here to tell you something very important to your life. As Charles stop speaking, Joyce knew this was not a joking matter anymore, can someone tell me what I need to know please, I'm dying of too much suspense, spite it out please, I can handle it.

Now more than ever before, kanga took the bull by the horn and shocked everyone. I am your biological father and this woman here, Eliza is your biological mother! We are sorry for what I let you go through in your life, I guess I can never make up for it enough, but I am willing to try if you forgive me. Kanga is my name from Kenya back in Africa. I met your mum in the high school back in our village where I was her class teacher and one thing led to the other, she became pregnant by me and I was not man enough then to stand by her. His face bent down wards in tears and shame, for a moment, he was silent, everyone in the room was too but Eliza broke that silence. My child, please forgive us. I was too young to fight for you, then I had nothing to give you away was my best option, but now, I am not ready to let you go again. Ever since the day I held you last in my arms, your memories have always been with me. They are the oil I use each day of my life to light the lamp of my life to this day. Please, never feel rejected or abandoned, we do love you greatly.

After I got back home, I contacted my mentor who raised me when I was rejected and banished by my people who felt I committed a crime against them for getting pregnant before marriage. I ask her about the way you were adopted and by whom. From the story she told me, I knew you were my lost child instantly. I had not seen your father ever since, as you can see, I am happily married with three other children to my husband here, Charles. He has been my pillar of strength since then. We found your father here, only few days ago and here we are, please forgive, it often said that to eerie is human and to forgive is divine" please my daughter. The reaction as well as the news for Joyce was mixed, she never knew this day will come not in the way it did at all. All through her life, she wondered who her real parents were, she wondered what motivated them to throw her away to be adopted like she did.

Above all, she wondered why she was not loved enough by them to fight for her. Now she understood better the circumstances surrounding her birth, adoption and eventual life, she is seated face to face with the original persons who brought her to life, her only option is to accept and forgive and give thanks to God for a day like this in her life. She is happy that they found each other before their deaths. That was how Eliza got her granddaughter to come spend her holiday back with her in Africa before the kidnap. At this point in kanga's life, the incident triggered in him a new beginning, after the hugs, handshakes and kisses from all, then Eliza settled down home with her family. Joyce became a regular caller to her mum in Africa, she was not too happy because her adopted parents both died in a terrible car crash two summers ago. She became more relaxed to find them at this stage of her life. Back in her home, madam Remi remembered her life. She remembered her growing up and her story which led her away to find her husband in Kenya.

She had a similar story to tell about her life in Africa where she comes from, whenever she sees Eliza, many memories of her life reflects in her mind. Here is her life story, her father was originally from a city in Nigeria close to the border town of the river Niger in a very small oil rich village. Their home as in most village houses wakes up early at the cock-crow before dawn, the children of the house and other neighboring houses surrounding the village, each will wake up their child, dress them up as quickly as possible, the female ones will now balance large clay pots on their heads or those who prefer calabashes will tenderly carry them on their heads and walk many kilometers to the only source of water in the village stream. While the boys go hunting for any busy animal to make delicious meals from the water the girls fetch from the stream. The stream is actually a brook where the whole villagers bath, fills their containers with water, defecate on one corner of it, believing that as the stream flows, away it goes with whatever came out of them. This has become a routine for all maiden and youths of the village, this daily routine takes about one and a half hours for Remi and her friends who look forward to going to the village streams at the dawn of each day. When they return home with this water, each girl's mother will filter the water to remove any suspected parasites and then divides the water into three containers. One for household use, one for drinking and another for evening bath. Any washing of clothes must be done at the stream on the village market days.

However, during the raining season, the bottomless well which store up water from the flood serves as a water reservoir, where reptiles and other aquatic creatures that find their way into the well-constructed pit would die and get rotten inside. The unpleasant odor from these mud did not deter the people from drinking this contaminated water, however, strangers who came to work as missionaries, teacher's, Engineers, Revenue collectors and oil field workers in the nearby oil wells of the delta region of the town would prefer to boil and filter this orange-like liquid before they could drink from it reluctantly for fear of getting infected with water borne diseases. Surprisingly, no case of water borne disease had been reported in the village as it were.

In the village where Remi was born, all the male adult are true peasant farmers while their wives compliment farming with petty trading. The village, because it is located in the oil rich region between the borders of the river Niger bridge of delta state of Nigeria, south-south, it attracted more tourist and visitors who crave for the fortunes of a better life in oil. It was during this time that Remi met and fell in love with one of the oil worker who stole her away from her village and took her to the city where he lives. She went with him after his promise to send her to school in the city and give her a better life. Things warm up well for her and her lover for the first few years of their union, he indeed sent her to school after making sure that she will be his forever. After her primary six exams, Remi pass out with flying colors, her man was so proud of her he decided to celebrate her successes that night by taking away her virginity which he promised never to take until she graduated from the university as he promised to train her to that point. To Remi, education was one of the main reasons why she followed him down to the city. As she served his dinner that cold night, Paul noticed how beautiful she has grown this past few years they have been living together, the desire to take her to bed overwhelmed him in a different manner. How will I like such a beauty pass me by in my own kingdom? If I don't take her now, somebody else may do so and all my efforts with my investments in her will be in vain, I better be the first to take her before someone else does. After all, she is mine, I brought her from the village.

This thought filled his mind as he lay on the bed in the single bedroom home they share together, after this, he decided to put his plan to action by inviting her to share his bed that night. Remi, why are you lying on the floor today? Don't you think it is time you start sleeping on the bed with me? You know you are my angel especially now that you will soon go to college. Please come sleep with me here on the bed. No, Uncle Paul. I cannot. And why can't you? You know you always sleep there while I sleep here. I'm better off here please uncle. Don't you call me Uncle Paul again, I am not your uncle, I know we have been living like this, but it is only to deceive people until you are grown enough to make your own decisions. Now you are no longer small in size, but small in age.

Look, I am willing to do anything to make you believe me when I tell you I love you. Do you think I stole you away from your village to keep as a pet or what? I want to train and marry you. As for me, I am not getting any younger by the day. The way things are I might go away from you if that makes you feel better. She wondered what he meant by all these words. Since she did not want him angry, she decided to give in to his demands. That night, she lost her innocence, she gave her virginity to Paul and that was the beginning of the end for her. Few months later, she discovered she was pregnant, the news to Paul was a big blow. Unknown to Remi, Paul is a polygamist with children back at his village in koko area of the delta. He has two other wives and six children he left behind in the village. He goes to see them some times while he started another life with Remi unknown to any of the other wives in the city. He managed this secret until the day Remi gave birth to a baby boy. After the delivery of the child, Paul simply vanished into thin air. She came back from the hospital to meet an empty house, that day it was when her world came to a standstill. She survived by the help of her neighbors and friends she made who knew all along that Paul was married with children in his village.

All attempt to locate him proved abortive. He left his job with the oil company, vanished into thin air and never bothered what became of Remi and his son, unfortunately, the child died at six months old of an attack from measles. She never had the means to give him good medical care. She on her own survived by following a caterer who gives her food and shelter at the end of each day. It was there she learnt catering and later met a Kenyan man who visits her madams' restaurant for food each day. She married and followed him back to Kenya but never had a child again in her life due to complications from an infection she contracted after the birth of her first child. It was this story that motivated her to assist Eliza (Ada). That evening, as soon as carol got back from work, she met Richard her husband watching the 9pm news in the living room. She walked passed like someone in a hurry and quietly shut her bedroom door from behind. Richard did not know what to do. He has persistently wished for a better deal from his wife carol, but the idea of separating himself from her, gives him the chills like nothing else. However, this relationship cannot remain like this forever. Daddy, is that not your wife who just entered her room? Are you going to speak to her or you want to remain like always here alone? Maybe I should see things from her point of view. Your dinner is severed on the table daddy.

April concentrated on the car parked few kilometers from across the street facing their house, she has been wondering why the car has been there without moving for over an hour. She saw a man looking through the window of the car to their house, but did not see his face well enough to recognize him. 'I wonder why that car is still there. Maybe I should go tell dad if he can check it out. Oh, I forgot, daddy is not the right person to go to now, she voiced it instead to Sam her brother who now decided to go with her. Let's check it out, both grabbed their coat and went out the door to the street down the road. As they approached the car, Dean slowly worn down the car side door mirror. Hesitantly, he step out of the driver's seat and stood waiting to meet carol's children. For the first time, dean felt like a caged bird again. Seeing this two children from the woman he loves makes him want her the more, he imagined them to be his. What will he tell them? Are they the key to his success with winning the love of their mother? Will they ever accept him in their lives as a step- father if ever their mother accept his love, but what kind of man is their father, Richard? Will he give this all up to me? Well, he enthused that it is only time that will tell. Hi, can we help? We noticed your car have been here for a while, do you need help? Dean saw in April, the image of the woman who has stolen his heart.

He decided to use the opportunity before him now to achieve his aim here in the city. Hello, my name is dean. I 'm looking for someone. I mean I am looking for the house of Mrs. Richard's house. Do you happen to know where that is? Sam and April stared at each other, it was as if they suspected Dean was not really harmful. His good looks with his aristocratic dress sense won them over to suspect him of any danger. As he looks ahead to meeting their mother, he decided to push this luck further. You look exceptionally like the woman I am looking for. Are you guys related? Actually, she is our mother. Why do you want to see her? Well, I am here for good. I have an important message for her. Can I see her? Why did you not go see her in the office? I did try young man, but they would not let me see her. I was told she does not see anyone, except on appointment and this is so very important for her and her country, so here I am. Instantly, april voiced out her disgust for her mother's high handedness.

As always, my mother is too important to be seen by anyone, without an appointment. Sorry, it's just a slip of my thought. Am not supposed to say that a loud. We don't know if she would still see you now without an appointment. Even now so, coming this late to her house, but we will try and see what we can do for you. But, we are not promising you anything. Give us the message let's take it to her if she would oblige you. Sorry guys, I can't do that. This message has to be delivered personally by me. It is too important to let go indirectly to her, besides, she has to give me her word back to the country where I was sent. Ok, you mean you are not from her? No, I travelled from a very long distance to find her. This is how important the message is, please no insult intended. Right, then we will go inside and see what we can do for you. What is your name at least? I said that before, Dean. Tell her a message from Kenya. She will understand. Thanks. Ok, wait here, we will be back. As the children went back inside, April's mind waved through the cute handsome guy and the charismatic way he spoke to them.

She wondered if her mother would see this man at all. Since her arrival back home, April and Sam have not seen or spoken to their mother. They have seen her from a distance in the house, but never said hello. The anger from them towards her has made it impossible for them to have a better relationship with her. Anyway, they first approached their daddy in the living room to tell him about the man outside looking for their mother that night. Daddy, there is a man outside who wish to see mum. He says it's important. What do we do? Richard did not mind her, he reluctantly waved his right hand with his eyes still glued to the news and said' she is in her room. You can go and tell her, I don't think she would want me to say anything to her visitor. You know she is the boss here my child.

April and her brother Sam shook their heads and walked to their mother's bedroom to knock at the door. Knock, knock, mum, there is a man outside who wish to see you. Knock, knock, and can you here us? You have a visitor outside who wish to see you. He said it's very important. He came from Kenya see to you with an important message. That word Kenya got carol off her feet, by now she was already lying on her bed lost in her thoughts. She understood quiet well what that word meant, it brought back surging memories for her. In her mind's eyes, who on earth could have come from Kenya looking for her this odd hour? Nobody knows my house, but how, how did they get here? She knew that it couldn't have been Mr. Kanga. Kanga cannot come here. He cannot come looking for me, we are not friends. But who could this be? The desire to find out who the interesting night visitor is outweighed her pride, she eventually gave into her thirst for curiosity. Her children to her are problem of their own. Their constant reaction interferences and conduct towards her problem with Richard gives her much concern. She know they always take sides with their father against her, to her, it is not their business what she does with their father. But she will keep that aside for now and find out who the uninvited guest is at this time of the night. Who is there? Mummy it's us, April and Sam your children. I would be out in a minute. Ok. She put on a silver night gown with flowing ribbons and red buttons to the top of her breast.

The sleeping gown accentuated every contour in her body, showing off the beauty in her which she still maintains even after the birth of her two children for Richard. Stepping out of the hall way, she saw her husband looking at her ravishing body in the sleeping gown. His mind went back to the first night he made love to her, back in the university. She wore a similar gown that night when he couldn't take his eyes off her. Today, seeing her in a similar gown brought back memories of the good time he had with her. His hunger for sex with her she could see in his eyes, for a while, she felt for him. She would love to have sex with him but her ego and memories of what happened in that Kenya hotel room with dean has taken away that hunger for sex from her. Now especially, her body only hungers for Dean's love. Hi, who did you say is looking for me? She ask. Mummy, there is a man from Kenya who says he has an important message for you. Why is he her in my house? Who gave him my address, he should see me in the office! Can you just for once, see who he is? The man will not come here if it isn't important. Madam, for the love of god, please see who he is. Richard said to his wife out of frustration from her naggings to his children.

Daddy is right, we cannot answer those questions for you mum. Only he who is here to see you can, so, please excuse us. Both Richard and his children ignored her ranting at this stage when they realized she was out to pour venom on them as usual. Reluctantly, she walk to Sam's room and ask him to usher the visitor into the living room. The moment he set foot into the living room and carol saw it was Dean, she lost her composure. Her heart beat increased rapidly. She gathered whatever is left of her pride and manage to speak. You? How on earth did you get here? Well, Richard meet Mr. Dean Almond. Dean, my husband Richard. Please to meet you at last Mr. Richard, I have always wondered about you, oh, no, I mean I have had so much about your good family. You must be proud to have such a lovely woman as a wife. Yes, sure thank you. I will beg your excuse now please, I have urgent matter to attend to inside. Please to meet you once more. Unknown to dean, Richard's life is in shreds with his marriage to this woman, but before the eyes of the world, they see him as lucky as can be to be the husband of carol. Only those close enough know what hell he lives in with her. He shook his head regretfully again and went straight to the loneliness that is this life of his.

Carol focused her attention on dean. Dean could not help his sexual nuttiness. Haven tasted from this poisonous triangle before, seeing it again inside this transparent sexy night gown brought back memories of the past with her back at the hotel in Kenya. It is this forbidden apply pie of carol that has tormented and driven him as mad as to take the crazy risk he takes just to see her again. Can you stop? Take your eyes off my body. Do you know you are crazy? Why did you come to my house? Do you want to put me in trouble? I told you that was a mistake, yet you came to my house? How on earth did you find me? Oh come on, give me a break please. I am here for good. I came to the office drop my number but you never called. Please, see me tomorrow at the office by 9am. I can't take this no more, this is my home. Ok, let's meet at this place take this address and meet me after work tomorrow. I promise you it will be worth the while. Please don't keep me waiting, I have an important message from Mr. Kanga for you. He dashed out the door as fast as he came inside. His mind at rest, he knew there and then that there is still hope for him with this woman. Dean saw in Richard's eyes what another person has not taken time to see.

He saw the regrets, and the pain of a lonely man in him. That night, back at his hotel room, he felt relieved and accomplished seeing carol again. He knew he has conquered this woman's love, from the way she reacted after seeing him for the first time since the night he made love to her back in Kenya, he knew undoubtedly that she will show up at his room the next day after work. Either out of curiosity or want for him, dean awaited her arrival that evening. With a green combat short and a black matching shirt with sandals on his well manicured legs, he sat gaily on the bed by the third floor window waiting to see her walk through the door straight to his arms. Surprisingly, there she was looking down on him right in his room. How did you get in? I thought I locked the door? I didn't hear you knock. Well, you forgot to lock the door so I came in quietly 3minutes ago. You were carried away too much in whatever you were thinking off and you never noticed me come inside. What else could I have been thinking of if not you my angel? He got up from the bed attempting to draw her close to his body as he did before in Kenya.

She pulled away quickly. Dean, I did not come here for this. What happened back there is not real. We can't let it happen again. For me it is as real as day light, it will always be real with me. I looked for you all over Kenya, why did you go away without telling me. You never finished your business with kanga and you left. Is it because of what happened between us? No, that was nothing. Are you sure that was nothing to you? Your eyes tell me a different answer. Why are you trying so hard to hide this love? In love, there should be no pride, but I can understand. Today after seeing your family, I realized that I have been wasting my life pursuing irrelevant things of the world. With all the money, connections and all, I just realized that without somebody who truly loves me, I am as formless as the wind. Now, you have brought back in me, that feeling of family, with the urge to love and be loved in return and children as a better priority to wealth. I have realized with your help that I need a better life than what I now have. I want carol, to share my life with you. I don't mind to remain as one of your family if you allow.

But I confess, I AM MADLY IN LOVE WITH YOU. Carol's eyes wide open, to see Dean begging for her in this manner is like breaking Mr. Kanga's pride back in Kenya. Unknown to her, the best is yet to come from this guy. What do you expect me to do Dean? Of course you know I'm already married, I advise you to stop feeling this way for me. I can't give you what you ask, I am already too committed with my family, but----. What? Say it please. Don't turn me down again carol, please. She turned around, with a deep feeling of satisfaction. Knowing in her heart that she cherish this moment of her life, another desire to conquer this man's heart as an adventure to her began thumping in her head. If you give me time, I will think about it. Let me know what risk you are ready to take for you. As you know, my husband and children are there to be considered (she just said this to give the impression that she cares for her family when the opposite is the case), I have great love for them.

I know this much carol, but they can also be mine if you want. We can make a better life together carol. I will make you very happy my love. He put his arms around her waist again in an attempt to have his way with her. While she desired this affection, she did not know when again Dean put his lips on her willing mouth and again they made passionate love more than they did in Kenya. For the next 1hour, Dean and Carol forgot who they were. The passion from both heart was so intense it took away fear from both. Never did they realize how much they meant to each other until this second moment of intense love making. As it were, dean has conquered her in her own doming. He has conquered the lion in its kingdom! He never thought it would be possible again to have this lioness in his kingdom, but it has happen again. This is great hope for him never to give up on this love.

Her heart is willing but the flesh is weak for her. Carol felt like a princess whose prince charming has come to rescue for the tower of the evil queen. Now, she much have to decide which way to go in her life. Although, the idea that she and Richard would separate never crossed her min. as for now, there is every possibility for her to run away with this man, Dean, who has stolen the sexual passion of her life. She has more or less become a sexual slave for this man. Something she never thought possible in her life. Unknown to Dean, Carol is ready to submit to him any time he touches her. Sex is the only weapon dean can always use to conquer her. This weakness, she is determined to hide from him as much as possible, if she can. Still basking in the euphoria of sweet love making, she got up from the bed and quickly dress up to go. The clock in the bedroom, as she raised her head to look, was already at 12midnight.

She then realize how late it was to drive home to her family that late at night. Pretending to be worried, she made attempt to make dean feel guilty for keeping her that late. See what you did, how can I drive home alone this late to my family? I told you I don't want to go through this again, but you wouldn't listen. What do I do now? Sitting beside dean's naked body on the bed, her eyes against her wish, roved through the raw strength of this handsome man, sleeping like a baby satisfied from mothers sweet breast milk.

She put her hands on his hairy chest, stroking with one finger up and down the navel region. She imagined those sexy hairs touching her naked body when they make love. Wondering how far this story will get, she once again wished to be his forever. The stroking woke up Dean. Hi baby. Are you up? It's just too late to go home. Why don't you pull off your clothes and come sleep beside me here on the bed. Come sleep on my chest let me put you to a good night rest. Dean, look at the time. You made me do what I have never done before, not even with the father of my kids when we were dating. Honey that is what we call "the power of love". You are so in love with me as I you. Come on, let's enjoy this night together, please. Up to this point, dean has not told her what he came with for her. He wanted first to establish that they have a relationship to satisfy his own needs before the kanga good news for her carrier. Giggling like a young school girl in love, still pretending to be worried, carol was more than delighted to spend the night in dean's arms. Ok, but what will I tell my husband? You know how to handle that, after all, you are a smart lady and your husband looks gentle. Please, forget about him for now, you are all mine tonight. I don't want to share my moment with him or any one.

She smiled and fall back on him in the bed for another round of hot sex. Even though he knew she never returned home last night, Richard knew there was nothing he could do to his wife whenever she returns. His greatest fear is for her to be safe. As for him, the idea of a confrontation with her is never an option, like most men would do, Richard never had the mind to stand up to his wife over her behavior. He does not even know if this attitude of his is normal or a sign of stupidity or all of the above. Sometimes, he sees himself as the woman in this marriage and his wife the man of the house. Could this have been the reason why their marriage degenerated so much? Is that the reason why his wife rejected him? Well, these thoughts filled his mind as he never know when he slept off with the heaviness as always. It was the sound of a car approaching the drive way of the house, towards the garage that woke Richard up from his sleep that morning. He looked out through the bedroom window, he saw carol, his wife stepping out from the car.

She carried her pocket book bag from the passenger side of the car, locked the car doors and walked to the door. As she approached the front door, she looked up the window to her left and saw Richard peeping miserably from between the window blinds. She smiled at him and fearlessly walked in to get dressed for work. She had given dean an appointment for later that afternoon in her office towards launch hour. Inside the house, Richard waited a few minutes for her to come out from her room and approached her. I can see you did not come back last night. Does that bother you Richard? No, I was only praying for your safe return. Good, you have no right to worry or ask me when I returned home anytime I went out that door. You and I know what this marriage is all about, I do not need to remind you again Richard that I hate it when you question my authority. I have too much on my mind right now, so please excuse me, I'm late for work. Like a stature glued to the floor, Richard stood for a few minutes on the spot where she left him. Not knowing what to do or how to react to another round of insult from his wife, he wept like a baby again. The truth of the matter is that, this man is bound to the slavery of a promise made. He sees only the fulfillment of the promise as his ultimate goal in life.

The problem now is- this attachment to this promise has turned his entire existence as a whole, upside down! This woman has crossed the line! But what can I do? If I turn my back on her, I turn my back on my late mother. I gave her my world in her dying bed that I will never lay my hands on a woman, no matter what. But I am dying gradually from this torture, why? Why did I put myself in this mess! It would have been his desire to turn back the hand of the clock when faced with the kind of maltreatment Carol gives him. The only thing left for him is to live with this for the rest of his miserable life, but, will he? As time went by, Richard realized the need for him to seek urgent help,. He decided that it was time to heal himself and become the man he once was but the first thing he said was to return back to talk to the only one person the finds peace, love and acceptance from. That person is his late mother, he developed the habit of visiting her grave whenever he is at his lowest esteem to pour out his b bleeding heart. That morning, as soon as carol left for work, Richard booked his flight and went back to the mausoleum where the remains of his mother laid in peace. It was like a new person finding his place of belonging, as soon as he entered the cemetery, he felt the stillness of the place. He wondered how lucky the dead were, resting peacefully in their various tombs with nothing at all to worry about.

Comparing the kind of peace they have to the hell on earth he now lives in with a wife like carol and the burden of a promise he made to his dead mother. Richard realized that life is but a passing shadow. It lives you with little or no options sometimes to the point where you feel like taking your own life for good to find the kind of peace which only you alone understand. According to some, the tears of the man in the rain, is only known to him alone. It is only him who knows how he feels right now. He sat down on the tomb stone in the cemetery, put his hand on his face and cried like never before. Calling out his mother's name as he cried, Richard was at his most vulnerable state this day. He played back his happy childhood days with his mother. He remembered how she would visit him at school in the elementary period of his educational stage. She would come at intervals to check on him, make sure he is alright before going back to her bakery store. Sometimes when she visits, she comes with some cupcakes freshly baked from her bakery for some of his teachers who looked forward to it each time she visits.

Because of this gesture from his mother, Richard became one of the favorites in the school. The teachers looked and cared extra for him because of his mother's sweet cupcake gifts, the most memorable of all is when his late mother picks him up in her arms, tenderly part his sweet face with her handkerchief and tell him these sweet words, Richard, it is going to be alright. You are going to grow up andmake me a happy mother someday, I wait for you my son to give me back my life in the joy you will give someday soon, my son. Where now he wondered is that same sonorous voice? Where is that strength that mama talked about and saw in her little man who is today a father and a husband? As his step back into his car, Richard decides to take his destiny in his own hands.

He decided it was time to stop crying and do something about his life. The sky was bright this morning, mr.kanuga woke up from his bed feeling weak and giddy. He could not understand what life has turned to be for him. Some where along the road, in the course of life itself, a man needs to take a critical look at himself. The things he did and the ones he should have done differently if given the same situation. He believed that the greatest miskate of his life, came the best thing he did and got from life. His child with ada, is the best thing he did with his life and the worst mistake as well. He regreted everything he did by that time when cowardice took the best of him. Oh! How I wish I could turn back the hand of this clock? He went round and round, playing the video of his youthful life in his head.

He rememberd vividly the first time he entered the classroom in the village and saw the pretty face of AdA, sitting very close to the window, staring particularly at nothing but lost in her own thoughts. Hi, I want you to answer that question? What question? Sorry, it looks like you are not with us in this class? Stand up, what is your name? Adaugo sir. Ok, Ada, I ask a question and you were not able to answer. Are you part of my class? Sorry sir, I was just carried away. Carried away by what? Do you have a husband or child that you are thinking about at you age? No sir? I'm not married or with a child. I just got carried away by the beauty of the sky and the good work of Gods creation. Oh, I see. You see me after this class, ok? Yes sir. That was the beginning of their fatal love story which defined the twist in the story of their lives. At this stage of his life, kanga knew he was drawing close to answer the call of his creator, but there is still a lot left undone to leave behind.

He thought it was time for him to put his house in order after his last visit to hie doctor where it was revealed he has a terminal disease which does not give him much time on eaeth anymore. Unknow to his family and friends, kanga has been suffering from cancer of the lungs. He has smoked all his life and drank the finest of wine and spirits whenever the occassione warranted, now, he has but himself to blame for what this has contributed to the rest of his troubled life. But first, he must make peace with the woman who bore him his first child and the one whom he hurt most in his life. He must beg the forgiveness of the child whom he neglected and rejected but who today is the apple of his eyes and the pride of his manhood, he has seen in his daughter the evil of rejecting ones own child, no matter the circumstances of their birth. It is never adviceable to deny a child you seer for whatever reason or circumstance as long as you shared your nakedness before that woman in the presence of not man, but God who sees all things. Tears rolled down his face as he pulled his weak body out of his massive bed this fatefull day. Kanga continued his thought in the shower of all that has happened in his life as he concluded that it was truly time to come down from this high horse he always rode to cover his softer side, the main thought of him dying without putting his house in order makes him want to cry the more.

The doctor told him that the way his cancer is spreding, he has less than six months to live. This is not an easy news for anybody to handle. How and when is he going to tell his wife about his secreat child? How will his other children handle the news? What will be the outcome if he decides to go to his grave with this deadly secreat of his life? Is he a coward afterall? All these and many more questions keep messing up his head as he truly look forward to his own death. He braced up for the worst and stepped out to do what he knows how to do best. Pretend in the face of difficult situations and feel you are totally in control. Kanuga know at this stage that the game is over. He saw from the back of his car the blue SUV car tailing behind him as he drove off from his street. Unknown to him, his personal assistant was on her way to his house that morning to deliver some urgent news from the new contractor who wish to work with the chambers in Kenya. Kanuga has never truly accepted that he would be as miserable as to not knowing what to do both in his private and public life when situations like this arises.

Driving through the parking garage in his office, he suddenly felt a sharp pain in his chest, he managed to park his car and as he attempted to step out of his car, he suddenly slumped and was knocked out. This was the last thing he remembered.when next he opened his eyes, he was surrounded by his wife, personal assistant grace who luckily enough was fast to find him slumped on the ground and quickly called the ambulance which saved his life. If help had not come fast, he would have said goodbye to the world on that day.t was Grace his very close personal assistant who requed him from the claws of death. He wished she had allowed him to died in his heart of heart so that his troubles would be over, but as the saying goes, if wishes were horses, beggers would ride" unknown to all, this man is dieing totally. He has no clue how to put his home in peace.

The sins of his past is now fuuly back to torment his life. As he look around him on his hospital bed, he decided there and then to die with this secret of his. He decided to take his regrets, mistakes and sins to the grave with him. Ironically, this is aman who thought to himself, the he was and is the strongest of them all. He saw himself as the symbol of African strength, but alas! When this moment come in his life, he rquickly realized that he is nothing more than a coward and a chiken at heart! Rolling his eyes from side to side, still trying to force a smile, he once again betrayed the coward that he is when his wife ask how he was feeling. 'My dear, I feel well enough to go home.

Unknown to his wife, kanugu is closer to his dieing days then where he is at right now. The burden of his guilt weighs heavely on his dieing heart. His life has been that of twist and turns which leaves much to the imagination of man. But the price to pay is now. Without much ado, this man has come to the end of the road with yet many unresolved miseries. He has played life more than life has played him, but here he stands between letting down his pride and facing his guilt or dying with his pride with buckets of regrets. At this point, his mind wandered back to an encounter he had with a spirit being. He remembered been ferried away in the forest, wandering without knowing how he got there. A woman came calling out to him from behind. Telling him he will be a star but that life will turn him upside down at the end. Could this be the moment? But he is still determined to pretend all is well and life goes on as it seem.there is so much to live for, but life will not give you that option to decide how long you want to live or when you choose to die.

Kanuga got back to his resting place in his spraling bedroom, opened his briefcase with his shaking hands and collapsed to his bed with his head tilting to the left and his face twisting like a crused ball. He suddenly realized again that he could not move his left side of his body. His eye balls started rolling backwards and his feets cold to the touch. He manage to let out a faint cry which attracted his wife, but before anyone could do anything, he went into coma and was rushed back to the hospital again! But as the wife approached the main turn to the lasttraffic light at the end of his street in panic drivng, she realized it was too late. Kanuga, the man the traditionalist, the husband and father of Joyce, took his last breath with tears streaming down his twisted face! How are the mighty falling! He died with so much secreats and troubles which will lead to other troubles for his family. His wife, realizing that he has died, managed to pull the car over at the road side and called for an ambulance, she cried her heart out but she felt peace from within because, she know she is free from 25years of slavery and betrayal and abuse from a man who was more of a dictator than a husband. Life for her now will take a different path.

All the pain from all these years will be nothing compared to the joy she is to experience from his demise. She called his office and broke the news of her husband's death to his close associate and confidant, his secretary, Grace. She knew more than kanugas wife. Everything secretive about him is only known to grace and for this, Mrs. Kanuga does not like her much. But she have no choice but to rely on grace to know more about her husbands secretive life. The death of this man is the end of an era.Apperantly, the family is now under her control. Most of her silent desires for her children will come to pass, ultimately, the wealth of her husban is her major priority. Unknown to her, this man is a man of many intrigues. The ultimate secret from him to her will be the discovery of his love child with Ada. Hell know not a woman,s fury when scorned by a man! But this man is gone with no proper plan forthis family.

Again, it is the wish of this traditionalist to be buried according toall his traditional rites. He had written a will, unknown to his wife and children and requested that he should be buried in his ancestral home next to the grave of his great grand pa with all rites and ritual beffiting a traditionalist like him performed. He left a copy of this will with his lawyers and sent one to the traditional ruler of hisclan. Upon his death, he told his lawyers and secretatry grace, to inform his clan head in kenya and let them decide how his burial should go. Even at death, he still did not accord his wife her rightful place to decide how he finally depart from this world! As soon as grace got the call, she knew her end has come, she knew she would face a lot of truble from kanugas wife and other people. Since she was his closes confidant, everyone would want to know something from her about him.The news of kanuga,s death quickly spread like wild fire, it went far and wild and the whole city heard about his death, some were happy he died and others sad.

Chapter 6

Following this development, the elder's council came immediately they were informed as is the tradition and insisted on burying him in two days from now. Mrs. Kanuga was surprised to several men visiting her in her home to sympathies with her. She amongst other things noticed the traditional native pot placed in the front of her yard as symbol to honor a fallen traditionalist. Upon inquires, she was told it was put there a day before by the clan head of her husband's village. She ask that it should be taken away immediately, but it is against the tradition. Anyone who dares will die! "Who are you to tell us what to do with our brothers' corpse?

I and the others are here to carry him home to his final resting place. Woman, this is no longer your husband or responsibility, we are the custodian of our culture and our brother left us a will on how he wants to be buried! I am chief Ikemde, the ozigizigi of our clan. I am here for his burial, so, step back!

This is not happening, Mrs. Kanuga could not believe what she just heard.

I am not giving up my husband to you vultures to devour! I am his wife and will decide what happens. If you guys like, put several fetish stuffs out there, it will not stop me. Look, for your own interest, i advice you stay away and let these people do their thing. I know this is what my boss wants, he told me so himself when he was with us. This was Grace, kanuga,s secretary who has been in the house watching everything taking place. Mama, my boss asks them to bury him. He has everything planned out before now and I am aware his lawyers will tell u that.

Mrs. kanuga broke down in tears again, realizing that her plans have all been messed up! She silently in her heart cursed kanuga and wished he rot in hell! Eventually, kanuga was buried according to his wishes in the traditional way and at the exact place he wants.

Indeed! The life of this man has destroyed the life a woman, who never expected what fate toss upon her. It has made her realize, that the events of our life, past, present or future, is ultimately the bases of our actions. To this very point, she will forever remember the sorrows of her life with this man. Somewhere deep inside her heart, she felt the need to burst out her frustrations on herself. She nonetheless believed that she was under a spell of her own. Howbeit, that she wasted a chunk of her life for a man who never saw any good in any woman? she asks. Again, her mind went back to the time she was a little girl in the village. She remembered one faithful night. On her way back from the stream, she encountered an entity who prophesied to her that her life will have many twists and turns. This entity, in the middle of a dark road, where there is a thin line between what was good and bad. Telling her about a life she never wanted to be part of. Here she is to this very moment, still wondering if this whole experience is real.

She turns around in the shallow space of her dark empty world, one finger under her chin, heads bowed down and tears rolled down her aging weakened eyes. As the saying goes, she remembered the sound of her mother's voice, echoing back form the other side of the world, telling her that " the tears of the man in the rain, is only known to him alone!

Alas! This die is cast for her in this dangerous world alone. how would she break this ice of the passing of this man that was larger than life? Who will teach her how once again to breath and live for herself? She washed down those tears from her dying old eyes. The old wrinkled face with blood shot eyes and a little to the right, little to the left she was certain she could learn to live happy again. What awaits these women in this story? Who will save the Whiteman's from their own coming tragedy? What about faith, trust, love, compassion, victory and defeats?

Only time will tell where this all ends----- Until then, until the morning comes a life again, and the moonshines her light from all of this darkness only then can they all find and make their peace--------watch out!

www.ingramcontent.com/pod-product-compliance
Lightning Source LLC
LaVergne TN
LVHW091604060526
838200LV00036B/990